Ethelbert F. H. Cross

Fire and Frost

stories, dialogues, satires, essays, poems, etc.

Ethelbert F. H. Cross

Fire and Frost
stories, dialogues, satires, essays, poems, etc.

ISBN/EAN: 9783337256104

Printed in Europe, USA, Canada, Australia, Japan

Cover: Foto ©Andreas Hilbeck / pixelio.de

More available books at **www.hansebooks.com**

FIRE AND FROST

Stories, Dialogues, Satires, Essays,
Poems, Etc.

BY

ETHELBERT F. H. CROSS.

THE BRYANT PRESS

Toronto, 1898.

PREFACE.

The contents of this volume include a number of stories and essays, etc., which have been written by the author at irregular intervals during the last few years, and some of which have already been published in periodical form—some of the stories in *Saturday Night*, the essays in the *Week*—the earliest in point of date being the essays, the majority of which were written several years ago. The essay on D'Arcy McGee (An Exile from Erin) appeared in the *World*. Owing to the exigencies of space these essays have been abbreviated in the present volume, and for the same reason it has been impossible to insert the " Scenes and Spirit Songs from Azrael," originally intended for publication in this volume. The essay entitled " The Great Days " consists largely of extracts from a larger paper on " The Origin and Destiny of Man." This and other recent essays of the author (including " A New Theory of Life," " The Unity and Eternity of Mind," and " A New Theory of the State," etc.) have not been inserted in this volume, partly on account of their length, and also because they deal with controverted questions in economics and philosophy, and might perhaps be more fittingly published in a separate volume than in one which, like "Fire and Frost," is intended for popular perusal, and appeals to the public chiefly on its literary merits.

INDEX.

The Splendid Soul.

THEY stood on a star together, the Devil and Mammon, and looked down upon the earth as it swung like a little apple far below in the infinite vortices of the ether.

"It is a miserable little world," said Mammon, surveying it critically, "an extremely absurd little world."

"Don't judge it by its inhabitants," said Satan pathetically. "The world itself is not a bad one, and if you are looking for a bargain—something really nice in the way of worlds—there is the very thing you want."

"But what are those little creatures crawling about on the surface of the little mud ball?" asked Mammon. "I don't want a world with vermin like that on it. Are they ants? Are they bugs?"

"Yes, hum-bugs," said Satan. "They call themselves men, I believe, but they are really only vegetables, for they spend all their time hunting round for stuff to put into little bags they call their stomachs. They used to be spirits once, but all the spirit in them has dwindled down to a little spark they call their souls, which they seldom use at all, and they seem deaf and blind to all divinity in earth and air and heaven. I had quite a romantic career down there myself once."

"So I believe," said Mammon. "That affair was badly bungled on both sides. Speaking from a purely business standpoint, I could never understand why anyone should try to save souls when he could buy them."

"Ha ha ha," laughed Satan merrily.

"Oh, you may laugh," cried Mammon, "but this is a practical age and there's precious little that cash won't buy. Now if I were going into the salvation business and had the financial resources of Paradise at my command do you suppose I would go about the salvation of souls in the old fashioned way with churches, preachers, crucifixes, etc.? No, not I. I'd take a run down to earth and make a straight cash offer for the whole outfit."

"Ha ha ha," laughed Satan.

"Do you doubt it?" said Mammon warmly. "Well I shall go down and buy them. If they value their souls so little, perhaps I won't need the finances of heaven."

So Mammon spread his wings and soared majestically earthward, landing at the corner of King and Yonge streets, where he assumed the form of a man and strolled into a newspaper office.

"I am thinking of buying up the earth," he remarked to the editor. "What will you take for your soul?"

"You will find it in the waste-basket," said the editor, "I used it for a week or two, but the public wouldn't stand it, and the circulation declined. Run an ad. into the paper and you may do what you like with my soul."

So Mammon took the editor's soul and passed on till he met a woman.

"Sell you my soul!" cried the woman. "Oh, ever so gladly will I. It gives me such awful discomfort just at the most critical moments. A soul is the only part of a woman which no one seems to admire. Five dollars, did you say? O! thank you—that will buy me a new set of teeth."

And, smiling artistically, she passed away, and Mammon proceeded till he met a politician, from whom he offered to buy a soul.

"Why, certainly," said the politician. "It is a terrible nusiance to me. I have been trying to sell it all my life; but you must take it subject to mortgages, and clean it at your own expense."

So Mammon took it, sadly, and passed to the house of the merchant.

"I have locked it up in my safe," said the merchant, "for fear it might get out and interfere with business. My soul is the only part of my possessions which I cannot reckon among my assets. Its use means commercial ruin."

Then Mammon took the merchant's soul, and pro· ceeded till he met a laborer.

"Sell you my soul!" said the laborer. "Ask me for something I own. I pawned that to the boss for a living. I'm only a machine, you know, for working and eating and sleeping. What do I want with a soul?"

So Mammon asked the boss for the soul of the laborer, who sold it to him gladly, saying :

"It is the only part of him I can't get any work out of, and it's always on the strike. You may take my own if you wish it, too. I never use it at all."

Passing on his way, Mammon met a preacher.

"Why, certainly," said the preacher. "Bless us, what do I want with a mind? Thinking is not part of my business. Everything is down in the book, you know, and besides the old-fashioned days when preachers required souls have passed away. When one has a fashionable congregation one doesn't care to offend them by parading one's soul in public. Put a mite into the plate and you may take the soul if you wish. This is a practical age, and I can't run a church without money.

So Mammon took the soul of the preacher and passed upon his way, and as he passed upon his way the news of his mission got abroad, and the people flocked to offer him their souls. And as he walked abroad he was delighted with the beauty of the world, but disgusted with the littleness of its people.

"They are not men at all," he said, in scorn. "They are worms—earth of the earth and dust of the dust— and the most honored among them is he who sells his soul for the highest price."

But he was amazed to find so sordid a people sur-rounded by so many beautiful things, and marvelled exceedingly at the beauty of the buildings, the wonder-ful pictures that hung on the walls, the charm of the poems he read in the books, and the divine and pas-sionate music that filled the world with melody and joy when the people sang like echoes the songs of souls unseen.

And Mammon called the people together and offered to buy their collective souls if every one was offered, but when the souls were piled in the market-place it was found that one was lacking.

"Who will not sell his soul?" shrieked the people. "Where is the crank who will not sell his soul?"

They found him in an attic with his pen between his fingers, writing divinest music—the dreamer, the poet, the thinker—who would not sell his soul. They took him to the market-place and tied him to a stake, and lit the fagots till the fierce flames crept up and burned his warm, white flesh.

"Now, tell me," said Mammon to the people, as they watched the Dreamer burning, "who made the world so fair? Who filled it with the glory of song and the frozen joy called art; the pictures that blush and glow with life; the marble lips that almost speak; the poems that thrill and palpitate in ecstacy of melodious meaning? Who brought into the world the sweet things that make life worth living?"

The people bowed their heads in shame, and pointed to the stake.

"It was he," they murmured, guiltily, "the man we are burning—the Dreamer."

The Dreamer opened his lips and smiled, and spake before he died. "I leave my spirit to the world," he said, "and Mammon is too poor to buy it now."

.   .   .   .

They stood on a star together, God and the Dreamer.

"What is that wonderful world below?" asked the Dreamer, as he looked at a glorious sphere of light which swept through the luminous aisles of the infinite, its surface thronged with beautiful spirits, who lifted their voices in passionate song, exhaling many colored waves of melody and light·on earth and heaven, and filling the universe with joy.

"That is the sweetest star of all," said the Almighty One, "the ancient earth, transfigured by your love and suffering, and peopled with the souls you saved from Mammon. Come, we will dwell among them."

Spirit—Sonnet.

WHOSE was the hand that bound me down
 In this dark temple of mortality,
 And with unkindest strength confined
 A living Spirit in a house of clay,
O awful Father of tremendous tragedy,
 Shall I not stagger to my feet again,
Who sleepless in the midnight of mortality,
 Shudder forever with divinest pain ;
And thou, O Earth, unholy sanctuary,
 Dark mother, on whose bosom cold I lie,
Clasp me not ever to thy breast so tight.
 Soon shall I rend aside thy arms, and fly
Home to the realms of divinest light,
 The white eternal mansions of the sky.

A Face on King Street.

WHERE had I seen it before—that face so strange and so familiar? Suddenly in the twilight it paused before me on the street—the face of a youth whom I had never met, and yet whose eyes as he lifted them to mine startled some slumbering memory to life and stirred my spirit with a sense of strange familiarity, a sudden recollection of vanished joys, and sweet companionship, and a secret shared in common.

"Hallo!" I cried involuntarily; "don't you remember—'

The noise of the trolley drowned my voice, but his eyes as he stepped on the car met mine, and there suddenly leaped to his face a look of startled recognition. Then the car moved on and he was gone.

Where had I seen him before? Not in this life certain‐ly, and yet I knew him well.

To-night as I lie sleepless on my couch in the still watches of the night, I seem to hear the sound of muffled drums, and my spirit is stirred to its profoundest depths by a sense of sweetest reminiscence. The corridors of memory are thronged with shadowy images imperceptible before, and a thousand deeper recollections, which form a shadowy background to the face I saw on King street.

. . . .

I know to-night that the life I am living is only one of a series. The spirit of man is eternal, and will endure for-ever and has forever endured. There is no beginning, no end—from birth to death—from death to birth, we

part to meet again, while fate behind the scenes sits spinning the looms of life and love, and binds our souls with
kindred souls in sweet melodic sympathies through the
long vistas of eternity.

In the sweet silence of the night the doors of the darkness are opened and the mystery is unveiled.   I see it
all again.

.   .   .   .   .   .

I was leading an army to battle on the plains of Issus,
and stretching far away before me in the gray light of the
morning I saw the gilded helmets of ten thousand times
ten thousand men-at-arms, their helmets flashing bright
in the sunlight, their gorgeous banners floating proudly to
the breeze, their legions forming for battle at the imperious summons of brazen trumpet and clashing cymbal.
See, they advance.   The armies meet.   The glittering
swords clash on the brazen helmet and shield, and steal
into the joints of the armor and drink the blood of life.
In the fierce death struggle the warriors grapple, and
with clinched teeth and uplifted hands they struggle
madly, fiercely, and the air is filled with the noises of
battle, the clash of the sword, the war-cries of the legions,
the shrieks of dying men and horses.   Ah, see! they
have broken our phalanx.   To the rescue, my gallant
Greeks!   Quick!   Remember Marathon.   At the head
of the last legion I plunge into the battle, but not alone.
Ah, no.   Who is it rides on the white horse by the
side of my gallant black as we ride gloriously forward,
thrilling with battle joy, our golden armor flashing in the
sun, the wild, hot blood of youth singing and dancing in
our veins, our bright swords glittering in a radiant arch

around our heads as we plunge into the battle and drive the foe before us like chaff before the wind? Ah, we were too fast. We are separated from the legions. I am surrounded. My sword breaks. My helmet is torn from my head. I am down. They are upon me, the enemy. Their fierce faces surround me. The swords and axes uplifted fall—upon whose shield? Who springs to my side and stands alone above me like a young lion at bay? They throng upon him fifty to one. He is wounded. He is bleeding. He falls upon his knee, still fighting fiercely, his shield above me. Ah, a rescue! We are saved! He falls into my arms.

"Hephaestion," I whisper.

"Alexander," he murmurs, the pale lips faintly smil-ing. As I lift the bloody helmet from his head the golden curls fall on my arm.

It was the face I saw on King street.

What does it mean? Who was Hephaestion? Who was Alexander? Where is the plain of Issus?

.   .   .   .   .   .

Another vision floats before my eye. Where am I? The lights are bright and the table is set with costly cups—it is a banquet hall. Around the table, heavily laden with choice dainties, rich wines, rare foods and golden ornaments, sit a company of stately warriors clad in costly robes. At the head of the table sits a giant, who towers a head and shoulders above his fellows and wears a golden crown upon his head, and by his left side a mighty sword is lying, and at his right I sit, who am his son. Noiselessly to and fro soft-footed slaves pass, distributing wines and foods and fruits on golden dishes to the guests.   At the end of the table stands a youth, and in his hand is a harp.   The eye of the king falls upon him, and he speaks.

"Sing, Sweet Singer of Israel ; touch your harp and sing."   His fingers fall upon the harp ; his silvery voice uplifted fills the air with the glory of song.   The waves of melody beat upon my soul and awake sweetest sympathies.   They thrill the spirits of the guests.   The wine-cups fall from their hands, their voices are hushed. Silent as statues they sit, enthralled, bewitched, fascinated by the charm of the wonderful song as it throbs upon the perfumed air in sweet melodic waves of love and joy.

He is silent.   They throng about him and crown him with flowers and laurel.   The brow of the king grows dark.

" He will be king," he mutters.

He seizes the sword and leaps to his feet, and the guests shrink back affrighted, but I seize him by the arm.

"O, Saul, Saul, my father, spare the Sweet Singer of Israel."

The uplifted arm falls to his side.   I lead the singer from the room.   Together we tread the streets of the holy city to find him a place of refuge.   His face is uplifted to mine.

"Jonathan !" he cries.

"Ah, David !"

It was the face I saw on King street.

.   .   .   .

What visions are these that haunt me as I pass on my way to the Forum, what dark forebodings of impending evil ? What omens of evil portent ? The cock crowed thrice last night and a glittering sword was hung across the heavens. The air is heavy with the odor of blood and the Tiber is moaning in its bed as I pass hurriedly on to the Forum. Why should I fear?—I who had led the Eagles of Rome upon a hundred battle-fields and earned the right to be her—— Hush ! Who would speak with Cæsar ?

Ah, I am dead ! They throng about me, the senators ; their daggers are buried in my flesh, and there is one among them—one face—he will not strike. I see him bending above me, love in his eyes, a dagger in his hand. O cruel blow !

" *Et tu Brute.*"

It was the face I saw on King street.

.   .   .   .   .   .

The shadows are vague—incoherent. Many ages pass dimly before me ; his face is framed in them all. We were courtiers together, and kings together. We were soldiers and slaves, poets and priests ; in courts and camps, and in the quiet of the cloister—always together. They burnt us together in Rome for loving the truth too well, and I looked across from my stake to his and laughed—we were divine. The ages passed. I remember that glimpse of his face as I led the Ironsides at Naseby. He, bonnie Charlie, was a Royalist. The ages passed, all moving to one tremendous consum·mation.

.   .   .   .   .

The night is dark—black, black, black. What flashes of light are these swift breaking in on the darkness ?

Hark to the roar of cannon and the clash of steel to steel, battle and smoke and carnage, and the lines of contending armies. Strange faces gather around me, outlined in bloody mists and smoke. It chokes me, the smoke. No, it parts. I see the eagle. O, memory tremendous. Sound the trumpet! Shadows! Tramp, tramp, tramp! Dusky regiments are marching behind me. I am advancing, ever advancing, over the hills. See the white snow! Who is it rides by my side over the hills—white hills? That face—shadows—battles of blood and carnage! Where am I? These burning sands—these pyramids—Ten thousand ages look down on him by my side. Shadows—darkness. Where am I? Hark to the trumpet! the rattle of the drums! I am leading armies to battle. See! See! O memory tremendous—the sun of Austerlitz, arising, falls on his face by my side. Victory! Eureka. I am the ruler of nations. See! the kings are kissing my feet. Shadows! Where am I? Hark to the tramping armies—banners! I am leading them on—flame and fire! O monstrous conflagration, the angels of God are fighting against me. They have kindled the houses of Moscow. Frost! Frost!—it is in my veins. My blood is frozen. Shadows! Where am I? Alone—against the world. Sound the trumpet! See the sun! It sinks! Blood, blood, blood!— I am choking in rivers of blood! Fight on! I sink—I rise! Sound the trumpet! Who answers? What, am I alone? Nay! there is one by my side. Ah! hark to the dripping of water on the beach. Shadows! I am leading an army again. *En avant! mes comrades.* Lift the Eagles—once the best. Throw up the dice again.

My spirit is shrouded in darkness and the skies are
ominous and dark—but still, advance—advance. Where
am I? Hark to the crash of the cannon. Bloodshed
and carnage again ! bloodshed and smoke and carnage,
and the clash of steel to steel. Advance the Eagles !
Victory is ours, my children, if we crush those thin red
squares. They stand—are they iron or granite? Plough
into them with the cannons. Crush them—shatter them
—rend them. Kingdoms and crowns and sceptres to
the men that crush the squares ! Hold back the Old
Guard ; not yet. See ! I am blinded by smoke. Say,
are they standing still? Ay—Old Guard, advance !
Crush me those purple squares. Veterans of Marengo,
Jena, Austerlitz, See, they are gathered around me!
We have held the world at our feet. Crush me those
Briton squares—it will be at our feet again. Sound the
trumpet. *En avant !* Hark to the tramp of ten thousand horsemen as they sweep like the whirlwind forward
down on the thin red squares ! Do they break the
squares? The smoke is in my eyes; I cannot see.
What ! they recoil ! Sound the trumpet. Just one
more charge—one more. Reform the ranks. Ah, who
will lead? Who? Whose face is this by my side? Who
rides away like a whirlwind to reform the shattered
ranks and lead them, lion like, forward into the jaws
of death? See, he turns as he gallops forward, and
I see his bright sword flashing in the air as he rises in
his stirrups and waves a last farewell. His voice, sweet
as a wedding bell, comes backward on the bleeding wind
out of the valley of death.

" *Vive l' Empereur.*"

.   .   .   .   .   .

Eternal surging of seas, eternal surging of seas, they break upon the rocks—no, they break upon my heart; they break my heart, eternal surging of seas.

.   .   .   .   .   .

Where am I? Ah, I remember. Sound the trumpet. Just one more charge—one more—*en avant, mes*—Eh! Did someone speak? What is the matter—oh, I remember—Toronto—yes, Toronto—for a time.

.   .   .   .   .   .

I saw him yesterday on King street and now as I sit here in the quiet of the night I can hear the fingers of fate weaving the loom of a still more magnificent destiny, shifting the scenes, clearing the stage, arranging the lights and preparing to lift the curtain upon the other act in the drama of being.

When I step upon the stage for the last great act of all--the crowning cataclysm of the centuries—the last tremendous war, well I know that ever by my side in summer sun or winter frost—in the dark valleys of rejection or on the towering mountain peaks of glory— forever loyal, forever true, I'll see—the face I saw on King street.   There is no beginning, there is no end, only eternity and the soul

> What if we die—we meet again
> On some diviner height of thought ;
> O listen to the sweet refrain,
> We meet again, we meet again,
> Beyond the tears, beyond the pain,
> Beyond the death that slays in vain,
> We meet, again we meet again,
> Soul of my soul—we meet again,
> In white eternal halls.

The Eternal Fires.

THE breath of God is on my brow,
    And in my heart the eternal fires,
Flaming forever deathlessly,
    Have kindled in my heart divine desires.
And thoughts that clamour for eternity,
    And dreams that shudder at mortality
Until my golden chorded spirit all afire
    With never failing passion for divinity
Throbs with great har monies—supremest ecs-
    tacies
    Immortal dreams, immortal love, immortal
    fire,
Great melodies, and a divine desire
    To rise like some sweet sun athwart the
    night,
And glowing through the vesture of mortality,
    Kindle the living universe with light.

Accursed Sleep·

A CCURSED sleep—what, must I close my eyes
   On all I love—on all that loveth me?
The ecstacy—the beauty, the delight—of earth
     and sky,
   And flower, and wave and tree.
And lips that laugh, and eyes that glow and
     weep
   With love's rare smile and tender ecstacy.
Shall I forsake them all, O time, and flee,
   To shameless bow my head in shameful
     sleep?
Nay, rather will I steal the night from thee
   And make each hour golden with delight,
And hand them down to immortality
   To thrill the hearts of men with joy and
     light.
Alone amid the sleepers, I sleeping not, will
     write
   With words that glow and flame and laugh
     and leap
Like merry little sunbeams through the dark-
     ness of the night
   To kindle brighter mornings for mankind.
Sweet rest, ye tired mortals, while I watch
     upon the steep,
Back to your kennel, night !—I will not sleep.

The Great Days.

ROM the summit of this great century whereto with tortuous steps humanity, emerging from the valleys of great tribulation and passing through the furnace of bitter experience like a steel finely tempered to mightier uses, has come to rear the temple of an enduring civilization and lay the foundations of a more magnificent destiny, we may pause for a moment to review the history and condition of the race, seeking a justification of the past in the achievements of the present, and a justification of the present in the promise of the future.

What is the origin of man? Has he arisen from the beasts or descended from gods? Has he fought his way from savagery to civilization or has he come down from civilization to savagery? They who have something of the brute within them may wish to trace their genealogy back to brutes, but they feel the god like stir within them will seek a noble ancestry, and the justification of their pride will be found in that history which, with its records of departed greatness furnishes a golden genealogy for the race. Back in the earliest morning of time, seeking the earliest traces of man we find them not in hatchets of stone or mounds of clay, but in the ruins of great civilizations upon whose broken pillars and carven walls there is written in indelible letters the records of civilizations earlier still. The first glimpses of man we get on earth shows him, not clothed in skins and warring with brutes, but robed in purple

and crowned with civilization, walking with an imperia
mien amid the temples his own hands had built,
and in the cities which his mind conceived.   The present
is bound to the past by a golden chain of civilization,
and glancing back from link to link we find the
greatest of them all in the very beginning of history.
From Britain to Rome, back to Greece, from Greece to
Persia, Assyria, Chaldea, Egypt, looking back through
the aisle of the ages we see the beacon lights of
mighty civilizations blazing on the summits of the
centuries where the sun of civilization is reflected in
the golden domes of innumerable cities, till at last
it rises magnificently before the eyes of men in that
wonderful sunburst of mythology which shows us the
splendid golden age, where man, freed from contagion
of error, reigned in the world like a god on his throne.

.   .   .   .   .   .

The men who walk the earth to-day have not attained
to the full proportion of their personality.   They have
not risen to their full intellectual stature, nor developed
the highest potencies of their being.   The conditions
of modern life have not been favorable to the development of the ideal man.   The cruel struggle for existence,
the sordid atmosphere of industrialism and the social and
industrial restraints upon the time and liberty of the individual have retarded his proper development and
called into existence abnormal and unworthy traits of
human nature.   The man of to-day is an intellectual dwarf, hedged, bound down and crippled by an
evil environment.   It is only now and then by fits
and starts, in deeds of heroism and words of love we see

the real man breaking out from the constraint of his narrow environment. He speaks in a language of love and kindly acts, we see him in the martyr dying for his faith, in the lover loyal to his love, in the father toiling for his child, in the patriot warring for his land, we feel him when we scorn the false and love the true. His is the voice called conscience, and his ambition is that aspiration which bids us rise to loftier heights than those on which we tread. Through the vesture of an evil environment and along the lines of history we catch these glimpses of the ideal man, existent potentially in all, but masked by his age and shackled by his times, and wrought by the pressure of an industrial environment into a deformed image of himself.

And yet the environment is not wholly responsible for imperfect development of the race. The masses of mankind themselves have proved too willing to bend their necks to the yoke and they sleep the sleep of mediocrity, instead of rising sublimely in splendid rebellion and asserting their mightier manhood once and for ever. To those who worship the beautiful and love unsullied light, who cherish in their minds a pure ideal, and keep their inner eye forever fixed upon the picture of perfection, there is something painfully repugnant in the continued mediocrity of the masses of mankind. It is mortifying to think that the majority of our fellowmen, in the very humblest of whom we fondly like to think there is something of the angel, should be contented neither to seek nor to soar but forever to dig and delve, to hoe and sow and eat and sleep and die. Yet this is the history of mankind. Untold generations have

done this and this only, walking forever with their eyes
upon the earth, oblivious of the stars. Sometimes, indeed,
they have sought variety in war and murdered each
other, and very often they have contentedly walked the
earth with halters on their neck, chains on their limbs
and darkness in their minds, bound by kings, bound by
priests, bound by capitalists, but above all things, bound
by their own consummate mediocrity. Only here and
there, and now and then a stately spirit has spoken, a
kingly soul has snapped his chains and soared, showing
that in human nature there was something of the divine
and whispering hope in the night. The history of
civilization is not the record of a race but the biography of an imperial few in every age who have risen
above the error of their age, lifting humanity with
them.

A contented man is a curse to the world. All
progress has originated in discontent. Civilization
itself was due to this. To be satisfied with anything less than the perfect is treason to progress.
The man who is satisfied with what he has will
ask for nothing better, but sleep the sleep of mediocrity, live a life of nothingness, and die the death
of a dog. The man who is dissatisfied will demand
something better, and get it. He will differ, he will
dissent, he will deviate, he will rise, he will reign, and
when he dies he will become an angel and aspire to be
a God. Discontent is the root of progress, the source
of civilization ; it indicates a lofty nature. The man
who is satisfied with the low, is low. The man who
aspires, complains and revolts does so because he has

something better in him than the things he sees without, and he seeks to make the world as perfect as his
thought.   He strives to make the lowly without conform
to the lofty within.   He measures the world by his soul
and finds it exceedingly small.   When old earth was
ushered out of the midnight of chaos into the dawning
of cosmos and passed from the agony of growth into
the bliss of completion, the spirit of unrest must surely
have passed from the element into the spirit of man
newly-made, and if ever it is banished from thence to
mingle again with the elements, then will be a fitting
time for it to sow the contagion of chaos again, and
kindle once more the cosmic fires to rend forever in
fragments the world whose citizens are worthy only of
its dust.   So long as men aspire, so long should they
live.   So long as the atmosphere of life is flooded with
hope and faith and the eye of man is bent forward seeking new vistas, new pathways, new light and new truth,
so long alone is it fitting that the sacred fires of life
should burn in his heart as on an altar supremely divine.

And so, forever tortured by divinest discontent in
every age and epoch in the history of mankind, there
have arisen from the ranks of humanity a few choice
spirits to lead the race to loftier altitudes of thought.
Without hope of reward, or promise of success, perse-
cuted, misrepresented, maligned, with hands that bled
by the roughness of the task, and eyes that grew dim
with a longing for the light, the master thinkers have
toiled in the quarries of the ages, hewing out the stones
with which to build the edifice of civilization.   The light
which lighted the steps of humanity on its tortuous

journey sunwards has been shone from the stake ;
where the hands of humanity, forever swift to strike, but
slow to save, have kindled fires to burn the men who saved
them. The happiest hour in the history of the race was
when the human intellect, turning from the profitless
disputations of an impossible theology and the eternal
nescience of metaphysics, sought refuge in the inductive
method, and science, the youngest child of the intellect,
was born to rise like a beautiful star above the horizon
of human endeavor, and, radiating light and heat on
earth and heaven, reveal the mystery of rock and
cloud, of plant and star and world. From the
birth of science the human race has advanced by
leaps and bounds ; the boundaries of thought have
been widened, and the tides of intellectual enquiry,
which formerly flowed in a few channels, now flow
in a myriad. Ideas, which were formerly the treas-
ured possession of a cultured few, have now become
the property of the many. The condition of the average
man has been greatly improved, and the number of
thinkers proportionately multiplied.

.   .   .   .

Reviewing the achievements of science at the close
of the present century we are compelled to the conclusion that the fundamental merit of its work lies not in
its conclusions but its methods. Indeed, science as
such, cannot logically attain to any definite conclusion
until its facts are fully accumulated, and the very system,
by which it proceeds in its search for truth by continually bringing new facts to light, necessitates a
perpetual modification of former conclusions. Theories

regarding the origin and destiny of man, the nature of matter and the relations of mind and body, which are based on the facts accumulated by science up to date, can only be accepted as provisional, and must be regarded, not as a declaration of faith on the part of science herself, but simply as the inferences drawn by individual thinkers from the study of the facts which she has accumulated and which are capable of other interpretations. The highest merit of science lies in its method, its rigorous insistence on a logical system of thought, its dispassionate ambition to acquire facts for their own value and without reference to the conclusions to which they may lead, and its reference of all debatable issues to the supreme arbitration of reason. Proceeding by this method the human intellect at the conclusion of the nineteenth century finds itself in the possession of a great number of facts, in the light of which the problems which confront it seem not incapable of solution, and which impel us to the conclusion that we are upon the eve of still greater discoveries, in the light of which, all existing hypotheses regarding the origin of man and his destiny must be very materially modified, if not entirely wiped out of existence.

.   .   .   .

The great days lie before us. The paths of thought opened out by the mighty intellectual pioneers of the past are broadening out into great avenues, and along which the children of men with ever quickening step are advancing to the heights of Utopia· In every department of thought we are upon the eve of great discoveries. The industrial problem, which has

been the chief impediment to the progress of the race
will be solved by a codification of politics and the establishment of a new state in which the people will resume
control of their own franchises, and in accordance with
the principles of a great economic law not hitherto
enunciated, socialism and individualism will be har-
monized, and national control of industries will be
reconciled with the highest degree of individual liberty.
But it is possible that even the establishment of such a
state may be rendered superfluous by the rapid progress
of science, and the possibility that the scientist will out-
distance the politician in his endeavor to emancipate
humanity from the thraldom of mechanical and industrial pursuits. The industrial problem may be solved in
a laboratory instead of in a legislature, and by a chemist
instead of by a politician. The chemist will solve it by
discovering a means of extracting the elements of food
directly from the atmosphere, where they exist potentially, as well as in the earth or plant or animal. Then
men, emancipated from the humiliation of mechanical
labor, will be able to devote their time to intellectual
pursuits, to the uplifting and the improvement of the
race, and to the solution of the riddle of existence.

.   .   .   .

Man is like a sleeping god. Only a portion of his
personality is active. This is the portion awakened by
the condition of the world environment, and manifested
through the five senses by means of which that fraction
of his great psychical personality which has awakened
looks out and takes cognizance of that portion of the
universe perceptible through the five senses. But the

greater portion of the environment and the most potent portion of it is supersensible, or in other words, it cannot be perceived by the five senses. As certain people are color blind, so man in his present semi-conscious condition is blind to all the finer formative forces of nature. Equally true is it that in the mind of man himself, and behind the senses as well as before them, there are great ultra-phenomenal forces and a mighty sub conscious personality. The vibrations of the ether from without, are not powerful enough to wake this to action, and hence unless aroused by an act of volition from within it remains dormant, and it only finds a voice in music. Music, purely *a priori* science—the science of numbers and vibrations—furnishes a clue hitherto overlooked by metaphysicians to the mystery of life. If heat, light, electricity, chemical affinity are musical vibrations of ether, and the mind could be made to vibrate in consonance with, or at a greater degree of activity, the thought waves might be correlated with ether-waves and we could mould matter into different forms by acts of volition.

.   .   .   .

Nature may be passive thought, as pictures are thoughts in canvas and statues are thoughts in marble, so also trees, flowers, worlds, etc., thoughts crystallized in matter. Now, passive thought is always subject to thought in action, and mind is thought in action, hence the mind controls the body. Hitherto it has acted only on nature, only through intermediate forces, but if the psychic forces and physical of the environment be correlated with mind, the latter can act directly on nature by thought waves modifying matter directly by mental action. All the so-called forces exist potentially in the mind of man, who is a microcosm of everything in the universe—divine and otherwise.

.   .   .   .

The thinker of the future will be a great musician and correlate the waves of ether with waves of thought, and modify matter by volition. Then will the god awake.

Scene from "Azrael."

THE DRAMA OF DEATH.

SCENE.—The Bridge of Suicides. Rosedale Ravine at Midnight.

Enter.—A man slowly walking on the bridge. He paces half
way over and leans upon the railing, looking down at
the ravine.

"WHEN will I hear them again, the voices of my dead? Out of this darkness will they come to me, or must I wait until eternity opens gates of death to me? Too sweet—too sweet—I think they were for such delay. There is a shorter, better way. Why should I linger in the world when love has fled? Life without love is like a world without light, night without stars or heaven without the dead. Wheresoever love flies there love must follow. And whether it be on earth or out of it, among the living or the dead, in darkest hell or brightest heaven, if God be just and truth eternal, love shall find love again.

"How dark it is below in that ravine. When last I passed along its pathway soft the place was filled with light. The grass was green. The sweet sun shone upon it and flowers blossomed gaily on its sward. A sweet bird sang divinely on the bushes—oh, ever so divinely did it sing—never before had bird sung quite so sweetly! It was the lark, I think—perhaps the nightingale. Ah, what does it matter, since it sang divinely—oh, ever so divinely did it sing! I think it came from Heaven, that sweet bird, so utterly divinely did it sing—but

never again, O God—never again. Who spoke of
Heaven? Did some one speak of Heaven? No,
it was flowers I spoke of—and a bird—a bird
that sang most sweetly.   Where are the flowers now?
Where is the song? Where is the sunshine? Alas,
when last I walked in that ravine love walked by
my side, but now love has departed. What wonder the
sunshine should follow, and the sweet bird sing in
Heaven. And underneath this bridge I seem to see a
dark ravine that leadeth to eternity. I think this is the
very path to Heaven. Shall I not tread it home to
those I love? Down in that dark ravine where last I
plucked a flower to deck my love shall I not find the
flower of love immortal? Yes! I shall put my foot upon
the railing thus and—and— Ah! what is that below?
I seem to see a darkness moving in the darkness. A
black-winged angel rises from the depths."

Enter Azrael.

Who are you?

AZRAEL.—I am Azrael whom men call death, and I
am kind to men. When life hath done with them they
come to me. I kiss them and they die.

MAN.—Kiss me, sweet death.

AZRAEL.—You have another love. What sought ye
on the bridge?

MAN.—I sought for thee and love.

AZRAEL.—Whoso seeketh for love must seek in lovely
places. The gate of suicide leads not to Heaven.

MAN.—Quick, shew me the better pathway!

AZRAEL.—Whoso seeketh me must abide with me,
but they whom I seek abide with love forever.

Thou Shalt Not Smile.

IT was Sunday in Tolonto the Good—Sunday of the year 2000 A.D. Throughout the city everything was quiet except where now and then a sacrilegious speck of dust, stirred by the wicked wind, made a naughty little sound ; but otherwise the city lay in silence, sepulchral and funereal, and everything was quiet—quiet—quiet.

Down in the Holy of Holies (formerly known as the City Hall) the sacred rulers of the city were gathered in solemn conclave, with tones subdued and manner reverential, discussing ways and means of increasing the sanctity of the Sabbath and adding to the holiness of men.   Long had they wrestled with their souls in violent prayer, with mournful groans and faces long and woeful, bewailing the errors of their fellowmen, and when the hour of prayer and meditation was over the Rev. Solomon Sorrows rose and spoke :

" Dearly beloved brethren, fellow-saints and sanctifiers of the city, the spirit moveth me in sundry places to declare and pronounce the wickedness of my fellowmen. Long have we labored, fellow-purifiers, to make this city holier than heaven, but, behold, we have not surpassed perfection yet ; for, oh, my beloved, it is not enough to be holy.   We must be exceedingly holy ; we must be intensely holy ; we must be very, very, very holy, brethren."

" O ! holy, holy, holy ! " groaned the brethren.

" Those of you who can endure the moral anguish of

reverting to the evil days gone by," continued the
brother, "will remember that a hundred years ago
Tolonto was a wicked, wicked city."

" O ! wicked, wicked, wicked," groaned the brethren.

" A very Babylon of cities was it, brethren. In those
dark days the people used to smile. Men walked abroad
with laughter in their eyes, and women wore no veils
upon their faces. The Sabbath lasted only for one day,
and street-cars ran upon it then, beloved. And, beloved, the city reeked with all abominations ; there were
theatres, and hotels, and cigar stores, and places of
pleasure, and libraries, where the people dared to read the
naughty, naughty, naughty newspapers, and wicked,
wicked, wicked books—books that were not written by
the Lord's anointed, but by the hell-inspired authors
who believed that life should be a time of joy and glad-
ness, that love was beautiful, and pleasure sweet."

" O! wicked, wicked, wicked !" groaned the brethren.

" And in those darksome, evil days, beloved, the people really had the nerve to think. They had ideas and
thoughts and principles not found within the sacred
Book, beloved, but born within their earthy, earthy
brains. They even dared to reason then, beloved, and
reach conclusions contrary to the Word, and contradict
their spiritual pastors."

" O! woe, woe, woe !" groaned the brethren.

" But the spirit of the righteous was avenged," cried
the Rev. Solomon Sorrows, exultingly. " We held a
plebiscite and we destroyed them. We formed associa-
tions of the righteous, and got control of the city. We
made a law extending the Sabbath for seven days each

week. We abolished all the abominations, the street-cars, the theatres, the cigar shops, the newspapers, the libraries, the museum, the ferry boats, the confectioneries. A law was passed forbidding women to go abroad unveiled. The public parks have been turned into graveyards, and none are permitted to enter them except to be buried. The Bible has been thoroughly revised and adapted to the higher spiritual needs of Tolonto. Thinking has been made a capital crime. Reading and writing have been strictly forbidden, and the colleges and schools have been abolished, lest the people might acquire or com-municate ideas not acceptable to their spiritual pastors."

"O! glory, glory, glory!" cried the brethren.

"Prayer has been made compulsory, and attendance at church is enforced on all classes of the people, who must spend twelve out of every twenty-four hours in the temple of the holy. All musical instruments have been destroyed, and singing and whistling are strictly forbid-den. Nothing but water is allowed to be drunk by the people, and a special law passed defining the kinds of food permissible, and the amount of butter to be used on each slice of bread, and forbidding the use of sugar, fruit, pastry, or other luxuries. When the people are not in church they are compelled to be at work, and the proceeds thereof go to the support of us, their pastors, the holy ones—the elect of the Lord."

"O! glory, glory, glory!" cried the brethren.

"All gaudy clothing has been forbidden, and the citi-zens must dress in crape and sackcloth. Silence is univers-ally ordained, lest the people say anything sinful. Pleasure-seeking is punishable with death, and local branches of hell have been established in the suburbs of the city, that the righteous may personally supervise the des'ruction of sinners. The sun, I regret to say, still continues to shine, and the wicked stars still twinkle sacrilegiously, and, owing to an oversight of the Lord, there are only ten commandments, which may be enough for certain places, but we want more than ten in Tolonto."

"O! more, more, more!" groaned the brethren.

"For, oh my brethren! it is not enough to be good, we must be goody goody, my beloved—"

"O Goody—goody—goody," groaned the brethren.

"And so, my beloved," continued the holy man, "we are assembled to-night to rectify the blunders of the Lord, and to make some additional commandments, and——"

At this moment the proceedings of the Council were suddenly interrupted by sounds of an uproar outside, followed by noise of hurried feet hastily mounting the steps of the temple, and in another moment a man burst into the Council and cast himself at the feetof the holy ones, shrieking and wailing and tearing his hair, and howling in heart-rending tones :

"O! woe, woe, woe! I saw him smile! I saw him smile! O! woe, woe, woe! He smiled upon the Sabbath!"

A hush of horror fell over the holy ones, and they gazed a moment in horror-stricken silence upon the messenger, till the enormity of the crime announced so violently dawned fully on their minds.

"Shut the door and close the window," shrieked the Rev. Hosea Scowls, leaping suddenly to his feet. "Let

not the news of the sacrilege get abroad. We will hear
the tidings in secret, and decree the punishment of the
sinner."

The door and window were carefully barred, and the
brethren gathered in sombre silence about the messenger, who was still weeping copiously upon the pavement.

" Who smiled, beloved brother ? " asked Rev. Jeremiah
Jaundice. " Open your lips, beloved, and say who did
this evil thing. Who smiled upon the Sabbath ? "

" Upon the Tolonto Sabbath ! " groaned Rev. Hosea
Scowls.

" Alas ! yes, upon the Tolonto Sabbath ! Who was
the wicked, wicked man who smiled upon the Tolonto
Sabbath ?

" Behold, I was expounding the word, my brethren,"
said the messenger, woefully. " I was expounding the
word to my congregation a little while ago, and had just
arrived at the eleventh hour of my discourse, wherein I
laid down the fundamental doctrines of the Gospel
according to Tolonto, wherein 'tis laid down that whoso
presumeth to be happy shall be doomed to eternal
damnation, both now and hereafter, but particularly
now. I was just expounding this holy doctrine, beloved, and the congregation of the contrite were receiving
the same as ever, with meek and humble looks and
downcast eyes, as becometh a congregation, when, lifting up my eyes, I saw a stranger at the back of the
church, dressed, not in sackcloth like our sacred youth,
but attired in gay apparel, and beautiful to look at."

" O ! wicked, wicked, wicked ! " groaned the brethren.

"And, behold, brethren, I watched that sinner care_
fully until my discourse was over, fearing he might steal
from the fold. But when I knelt down to pray the
appointed prayer for the eternal damnation of the happy,
I closed my eyes according to the law; but methought
I heard a sound, as though some one were stirring.
Then, behold, the Lord opened a corner of my eye and
I saw the youth depart from the church. Hastily I sent
messengers to follow him, and they followed him to the
outskirts of the city, where the wicked flowers bloom,
and there, beloved, he got on an abomination called a
bicycle, and he—he—he—— "

"Bar the window and stuff the key-hole," shrieked
Rev. Solomon Sorrows, leaping to his feet. "Stuff it,
stuff it, stuff it, brothers, lest the youth of the city hear
and become corrupted! What did he do, beloved?"

"He—he—he—smiled!"

"O! horrible, horrible, horrors!" groaned the
brethren. O! woe, woe, woe! Alas! for the sacred
city. Someone has smiled on the Sabbath! O! woe,
woe, woe!"

Then the brethren held council together in the Holy
of Holies, and made a new commandment :

THOU SHALT NOT SMILE.

And messengers were sent to capture the sinner.

.   .   .   .

He rode on his bike and he smiled. Out from the
streets of the desolate city where joy was withered and
love lay dead he rode on his bike to the sweet green
fields where flowers were budding and blushing and

blooming, and the golden dome of the glorious heavens, aflame with beauty and color and light, looked down divinely on fields that flowered and rivers that rippled and birds that sang, as the ancient earth, like a golden harp thrilled by the wonderful breath of God, quivered and trembled with joy transcendent and life immortal and love divine. He rode on his bike and he smiled, and the beautiful rays of the splendid sun shone bright in his path as he rode, and kindled the spring in the bosom of earth, till the voice of nature, melodious ever with breath of flower and carol of bird, smiled sweetly with him in merry greeting, and echoed the notes of his voice as he rode, with breath of bud and the song of lark and murmur of wave and wind and leaf. He rode on his bike and he smiled, and his joy was echoed in earth and heaven by a million azure smiles in the skies and a million laughing waves on the shore where old Ontario rolled her waters in mighty organ tones supreme, transcendent, and broke upon the shore with mighty laughters.

.   .   .   .

And so he rode along the countryside until he came to the beautiful park which the Council of the Righteous had turned into a graveyard. There, being tired, he lay down upon the grass to rest.

.   .   .   .

And as he slept, the darkness came upon him ; and with the darkness came the priests, its children. Like ghouls of the night, they stole upon him and seized him as he slept, and bound his tender limbs in chains, lashed him with whips, and tied him to a stake, and gathered round and questioned him.

"Why did you fly from the church?" asked Rev Hosea Scowls.

"I fled to seek for God."

"Why did you smile?"

"I smiled because I found Him."

.   .   .   .

They buried him under the soft, green grass, close to the heart of the nature he loved. And the sweetest flowers blossomed on his grave, and sweet birds came and sang beside the flowers. But in the sacred city all was silent. Tolonto's holy Sabbath ruled again, and everything was quiet—quiet—quiet.

A Guest of God.

THE lights burnt low on the altar, and humbly kneeling before the lights Brother Gabriel bowed and prayed, asking for light beyond them. Behind him the darkness had draped the church in gloom. Before him three candles cast light upon the shadows, feebly revealing in vaguest outline the chancel, the nave, the cross—and Brother Gabriel kneeling before it.

In humblest adoration he was kneeling, but in the holy place where holy visions come to the souls of those whose thoughts are holy, the thoughts of Brother Gabriel tendered earthwards, and dreams of earth were blent with prayers for heaven, and hopes of future bliss and joys celestial were shadowed by a memory of dead days and vanished faces. And even as he knelt in adoration before the altar of the church, his bride, his thoughts passed out beyond the altar, beyond the church, beyond the chancel—his thoughts passed out and knelt as he was kneeling before the altar of a love departed, and he could see a quiet little cottage standing beside a quiet country road, and he could see a boy and a girl together playing before the cottage, side by side. They had been lovers in their childhood, and lovers till a year or two ago, when he, surrendering to the wishes of his parents and to a sense of deeper duty, had sacrificed his love to his devotion and entered on his studies for the priesthood.

And now he knelt, a priest, before the altar of his
spiritual bride, and strove with inward wrestlings and
stern submission to hide away his craving for the
human and bury deep the memory of his love.   He had
thought it had been conquered long ago, that he had
conquered it, and surrendered it, and trampled it under-
foot, but the old love came back again to-night and he
could see a face behind the candles.   A year had passed
since they had parted, and he had heard she was
engaged to marry another—a wealthy and handsome
suitor named Victor Morell.   The match was a suitable
one.   Her parents decreed it and it was said he loved
her passionately and took her love for granted.   But
she—did she remember?   Did she forget?   Ah, what
a sacrilege it was to think these thoughts—and in this
place !

Brother Gabriel told his beads and strove to drive the
evil thoughts away, and it was consoling to him to reflect
that he had never erred except in thought, and that he
had ever lived a quiet, sinless life, shunning temptation
and ever devotional and abounding in good work.   Not
so was it with many others.   Victor Morell, for example,
who was addicted to drink, and gambled and smoked
and neglected the church, he could never enter the
eternal life, but Brother Gabriel, could he but erase
one little sin of memory from his mind, was certain of
his sainthood.   Brother Gabriel bowed his head and
prayed for Victor Morell.

.   .   .   .

" Hot Scotch."

" Whisky-and-soda."

" Old Irish."

" Lager."

" Whisky for me."

" Straight tip for Billy and cigars all around. Keep the change. Fill up, boys. Here's to you."

" Here's to Vic Morell. What's matter with Vic ? "

" He's all right."

" You bet."

> " For he's a jolly good fellow,
> For he's a jolly good fellow,
> And he's a jolly good fellow,
> Which nobody can deny."

With uproarious unanimity the merry company in the bar-room of the Red Lion tavern placed on record their opinion of the merits of Victor Morell in the words of the good old song, in which none joined more heartily than the enthusiastic Victor himself, as he leaned against the bar waving his glass and smiling broadly his appreciation of the good judgment of his companions.

" It's all right, boys," he said, somewhat unsteadily. " Perfectly correct in er'v particular, but guess I'll have to go."

A roar of disappointment broke from the meeting.

" Stay with the game, Vic," cried a companion pathetically.

But the opposition of his companions only strengthened the somewhat nebulous intention of Mr. Victor to depart for regions unknown.

" Got to go," he said, winking mysteriously. " Serious business—very."

" It's the girl," said one of his companions.

"What's the matter with her?" queried Victor, turning suddenly on the crowd.

"She's all right," roared his companions, and he passed from the saloon to the tune of the enthusiastic chorus :

> " She's a daisy,
> She's a daisy, etc. "

Mollified by this melodious tribute to his lady-love, Victor Morell staggered into the street. The cool night air, frosty and stinging, sobered him somewhat, and he vaguely realized that this was hardly the hour to visit his intended. Nevertheless, not caring to return and face the ridicule of his companions, he lit a new cigar and stalked majestically down the street in search of adventures. His mood at this moment was a decidedly amiable one. He felt friendly towards all the world. Everything impressed him very favorably. So far as he could see there was nothing the matter with anything or anybody, and everything was all right. He was surprised to observe that there were several moons in the sky, and that the sidewalk was inclined to be shaky, but still he made no complaint and assumed it was all for the best. The stars that twinkled in the sky, the snowflakes under his feet, the houses by the wayside, and everything, great and small, animate and inanimate, he reckoned among his friends. He was full of the joy of life, and living was pure ecstasy. Though not of a religious nature, he was even prepared to extend his support and friendship to the old church which towered at the corner ; and when he saw a light twinkling up in the chancel window he determined at once to enter and assure the proprietor

of his cordial and unqualified friendship.   Softly advancing he opened the door and looked in.   The body of
the church was thick with darkness, but dimly burning
upon the altar three candles cast a pale light into the
gloom, making the long aisles and the altar plainly visible and revealing the dark figure of a priest who, apparently absorbed in his devotions, was kneeling motionless
and praying before the mystic candle on the altar.   A
faint wave of incense carried his voice, strangely muffled,
to the ears of his visitor.

*Ave Maria, gratia plena, Dominus tecum benedicta, tu
in mulieribus, et benedictus fructus ventris tui, Jesus ;
Sancta Maria Mater Dei—*

The soul of Brother Gabriel was struggling with his
flesh, and in the quiet hours of the night and strengthened by the sight of sacred things, his faith was winning
battles from his love and hopes of future bliss were conquering ghouls of memory.   Afar from men, communing
with divinity, his spirit gathered strength to lose the
world, and in a dream of higher beatitude he thrust
away desire for the human and prayed for heavenly bliss
and life immortal.   He might forgive himself if God for-
gave him, and if forgetfulness were granted him in
heaven his love would be well lost.   And so with
thoughts turned Godwards and soul exulting in renunciation, he dreamed of the life beautific and——

"Can I offer you a cigar?"

The priest looked up in horror and saw before him
standing on the altar, a handsome youth in gay apparel,
a silk hat tilted back upon his head, and in his hand,
extended towards Gabriel, a case with some cigars.   This

vision, so profane and sudden, arising apparently from the ground, seemed to the strained nerves of Brother Gabriel like some infernal supernatural visitation, and startled him with guilty recollection that there had been a grain of earth upon his spirit. Was it the devil come in human guise, as it was said he used at times to travel to tempt the wavering spirit from the church? The thought possessed the priest with force of full convic-tion, and rising slowly to his feet and gripping tightly in his hand his crucifix, he held it sternly out towards the stranger, crying in thunder tones the exorcism, " *Retro Satanthe.*"

A merry laugh rang through the church, but the stranger did not vanish, but with a look of huge amuse-ment in his eyes, which even in the shadows seemed quite friendly, he sought to reassure the brother by remarking :

" I'm not old Nick, me boy—only a sort of cousin— dropped in from the external region to offer you a cigar.'

Brother Gabriel waved the gift away, viewing the donor still with eyes of horror.

" Satan or not," he answered sternly, " you are a child of sin and have been guilty of a sacrilege in coming here to-night."

" Well, call it sinner and be quick," answered the visitor genially.   " It's all right anyway, and as you don't offer me a chair I guess I'll sit down here."

He sat solemnly down upon the altar steps, still puff-ing at his cigar and contemplating the priest with much interest.

" You look rather glum, old boy," he remarked

sympathetically after a careful scrutiny. "Personally I feel gay."

"I am engaged in the duties of my sacred office, which keep me here to watch to-night," answered the priest with dignity. "Your presence here is a sacrilege, and you must depart at once."

"That's easier said than done," answered his companion amiably, "and I feel more like sitting than walking, but I *will* frankly confess to you I feel salubrious."

Brother Gabriel deigned no answer, but, standing severely erect upon the altar, he still glared sternly at the intruder, who, whether owing to the solemnity of his surroundings or the contagious sobriety of the priest, seemed to be gradually becoming sober and passing from a convivial to a philosophic mood.

"Funny thing—life, ain't it?" he remarked genially to the priest.

"Life is a sacred thing to me," answered the church-man sternly, "but you may find it funny now. Hereafter in eternal tortures you will reap the fruit of your carnal enjoyment to-day."

"Indeed?" said the visitor calmly. "Well I find it very amusing at present."

"But when you come to see the face of death you will repent—too late."

"Death is the episode which I look forward to with much interest," said the sinner serenely, "but I don't complain of life. And, by the way, what should I repent?"

"Repent of your carnal wayment of life, your cigars, your liquors, your cards; repent of your surrender to th senses, your love of the world, your scorn of spiritual things."

"'They all seem very minor sins," said Victor gaily, "and these are the little things that make one happy. The world is very beautiful and gay, but if you take away the flowers of joy, and drape the skies, and call all pleasures sin, why then I think it would be time to say fare-well—good-bye to life, and take a quiet sleep beneath the grass."

"'There is no sleep hereafter," said the priest, "but pain eternal for the souls who sought for joy on earth, and joy eternal for the whiter souls who did renounce the world, even as I."

A peal of mocking laughter rang through the church as the sinner rose to his feet and cast his cigar aside.

" What, you renounce the world! You have renounced nothing. How could you lose a thing you never found, or turn away from joys you never saw? What merit is there in renunciation that has not seen the thing which it renounced? The angels would disdain such craven conquest. Go out and see the world and then renounce it—if you can."

A troubled look crept into the eyes of the priest. Could it be true that he had conquered only shadows? Yes, it was true. To see the world, to feel temptation, and looking into the very eyes of sin to turn aside—that was what God required. He had but wrestled with visions.

" Go out and see the world," cried his companion. "See the sweet world, the world of joy and laughter, taste the red wine — wine, the lips, the pleasure.

Drink from the cup of life—life, purple, radiant; life as they live it out beyond the churches, where flowers bloom and bright stars glow and twinkle, and music, beautiful, profane, stirs the wild soul to rapture. Go out and see the world and then renounce it. You cannot, you dare not. "

"I can! I dare!" cried Brother Gabriel, with the light of fanaticism in his eye as he glanced towards the door. He had fought with shadows too long. He longed to go out and meet a real temptation and conquer it.

The sinner was startled to be taken at his word, and suddenly a strange idea came to his mind. Let the priest go back to the tavern, and he would kneel a little while before his altar.

" We will change places for a time," he said. " You shall go forth a while and see the world, and I will be the guest of God to night. Here, leave your gown and take my hat and coat. Go out and see the merry world this merry Christmas Eve—and then renounce it if you dare."

. . . .

The lights burnt low on the altar and the sinner knelt before the cross and smiled—smiled as he thought of Brother Gabriel brought face to face with all the world's delight. How different was that world from this dark temple, where the shadows had gathered so thickly, oppressing the spirit with gloom. He was stifled by the incense, and the white light of the candles hurt his eyes, which loved to gaze upon the sweet stars shining. And yet there was a strange, delicious pleasure in kneeling here before the quiet candles and resting far away from

all the bustle, the noise, the turmoil and the endless
striving of the wild world outside. A sense of spiritual
isolation, of mental peace and moral exaltation stole
softly on his soul, and he could almost think the darkness kindly that it concealed him from the storms outside.

"I could renounce them all," he muttered softly. "I
think I could renounce them all but one—she, never!"

" Gabriel !"

A cold shiver ran through the form of the sinner as a
voice fell on his ear—a thin girl's voice rising vaguely
out of the body of the church and floating towards the
altar, and lifting up his eyes he saw a shadow pass up
the aisle and glide towards the chancel.

" Gabriel," said the shadow, "are you there? I am
Marie."

" Marie ! " Victor shuddered—his sweetheart—here
—at night. What did it mean, and what was she to
Gabriel ?

He bowed his head and did not answer, seeming absorbed in prayer, but she glided up the chancel steps
and stood beside the altar.

" Gabriel, you must fly quickly," she said. " My
brother, who wishes me to marry Victor for his money,
has quarrelled with me to-day. I told him I loved only
you and would have no other, and he swears he will kill
you. O, you know his temper. I saw him at the
tavern as I came. He knows that you are here, and he
is coming O, Gabriel, if you love me hide somewhere."

The head of the sinner was bowed in his hands. He

did not answer. The joy of his life had suddenly gone out, and somewhere near his heart a little chord—a chord that once made music—snapped. What did it matter? It seemed the love of his soul had never loved him. What did anything matter now? Vaguely he thought of Brother Gabriel.

" He has gone forth to meet the world, he muttered, "and lo! his world has come to seek him here."

" O, God!" shrieked Marie. " Fly, Gabriel. Here he comes—he is coming."

A smothered curse at the door of the church as some-one stumbled over the entrance confirmed her statement. A man had entered the door and, glancing sternly about him a moment, strode fiercely up the aisle.

" O, you are there," he muttered fiercely, " together by——. Brother Gabriel, I want my sister."

The figure kneeling before the altar had drawn the woman to him.

" I am Victor," he whispered hoarsely in her ear. " Gabriel is at the Red Lion tavern. Now run away my pretty love bird and find your mate and make him happy. You give him love and I will give him life, and he will not renounce the world again. Run quickly. I will explain to Robert—and to God."

She turned and fled through the door of the chancel.

" Are you Gabriel ? "

A passion-torn face rose up before him, and a hand with a revolver met his eye.

" I am Gabriel."

A shot rang through the church, and with that splendid lie upon his lips the Guest of God entered a higher mansion.

.   .   .   .

"What's the matter with Vic. Morell?"
"He's all right."

> "Oh, he's a jolly good fellow,
> And he's a jolly good fellow,
> He's a jolly good fellow,
> Which nobody can deny."

The chorus rang out through the tavern, and to a man and a woman passing by there seemed to be an echo from the angels in the skies.

.   .   .   .

The lights burnt low on the altar, and softly resting before the lights the body of the sinner lay in peace, but the soul of the sinner saw a light beyond the lights that burnt upon the altar.

A Tragic Smile.

I dreamt a dream
But ah ! that dream is dead ;
It was a dream of things that may not be,
It was a dream of things too sweet to see,
And joy forever fled.
(My happy dream is dead.)

I am a dream
God dreamt———

T HE pen dropped from the tired fingers and the Dreamer buried his head in his hands, and with a heart as tired as his pen, and spirit ill at ease, he waited for the dying of the year.

" Let me in."

A voice harsh and discordant broke on the silence of the room and mingled with the sound of heavy knocking on the door. Rising hastily to his feet the scholar strode to the door and threw it open wide, and an old man, worn and bent with age, staggered feebly into the room and sank in a chair by the study fire. His face, wrinkled and furrowed with the ravages of time, seemed somehow strangely familiar, and his repulsive personality haunted the mind of the scholar with a sense of ghastly reminiscence.

" Who are you ? " asked the Dreamer, eyeing him wonderingly.

" I am the spirit of the past."

" No, you are not the spirit of the past," responded the youth dejectedly, " for the past is not a spirit, but a corpse. Who are you ? "

"I am the Old Year," said the visitor, warming his hands at the fire. "Let us talk together seriously. Your life has been a failure."

"You measure a man by his purse," cried the Dreamer indignantly.

"Yes, and I measure the purse by the man," said the Old Year severely. "But what have you done with your life?"

"I have done nothing," replied the youth. "but I have often dreamt divinely. While others, blindly practical, have passed their days in offices and shops, and lived the lives of vegetables and brutes, I have dwelt in mental palaces jeweled with happy hopes and golden visions. And day and night, by sweetest rapture thrilled, I have walked with the immortals on the Alpine heights of thought."

"But Joy dwells in the valleys," said the old man softly, smiling.

"Then she must dwell alone," answered the youth dejectedly.

"Tut, tut, tut," cried the Old Year sharply: "your life has been a failure and you know it. Capable of all things, you have proved equal to nothing, and now you must come away with me. We shall leave the world together. But first look at this mirror and see what- - might — have – been ——."

He drew from under his cloak a mirror whose silvery surface, as he turned it towards the Dreamer, was slightly blurred and clouded by vague and misty shadows.

"What do you see?" asked the old man.

" I see—a court-room ; the place is close and crowded
with men and women. On the bench, in robes of
ermine, a judge is sitting, and in the dock a prisoner
charged with murder. With tense, white face, hands
clenched and eyes despairing, his pale lips quivering
with a voiceless agony, he gazes hopelessly before him ;
while over his head, invisible to all but one, the angel
of death is hovering with hand outstretched to strike. A
witness is standing in the box, and near, before him,
clothed in robes of black, I see a lawyer (and the face
of the lawyer is my face). Hark ! he is speaking now ;
and his voice, stern and relentless, tortures the brain of
the witness until his jarred and quivering nerves, all
tangled and discordant, break down before the stormy
tide of words, and the red lines of perjury glow on his
ashen face. The witness descends from the box and the
counsel turns to the jury. He is reasoning—he is pleading. Over the twelve white faces he bends in a fever of
passion and pleads for the life of the prisoner. Will
they save him ? They waver. Will they slay him ?
They waver. With words that weep and thoughts that
burn and thrill he breathless bends above them plead-
ingly and cuts the quivering cords of doubt with sword-
like sentences of flame and fire. They waver no longer.
Eureka ! he conquers—the prisoner is free. The angel
of death has vanished from the court-room, and a soul
snatched from the shadow of the infinite. weeps on the
neck of his saviour."

" That might have been you," said the Old Year.
" That might have been you : but what are you now ?
A dreamer. Look again ! What do you see?"

"I see—a statesman. He sits in the council of the nation, and with a master hand and cunning brain he weaves the looms of history, and binds and blends the warring elements of race and creed and faction and religion into the frame and form, the pat'ern and pro- portion, of a majestic nation. I see him making history."

"That might have been you,,' said the Old Year " That might have been you ; but what are you now? A dreamer. Look again ! What do you see ? "

" I see an orator," said the Dreamer. " I see a mighty auditorium thronged with a multitude of people. On the platform stands an orator and he gazes dreamily for- ward at the surging sea of faces upturned, expectant, before him. In silence—nay, he is silent no longer. See, he has lifted his hand. Hush, he is speaking ; soft melodies are dripping from his lips. In silvery tones and sweet he thrills the chords of ten thousand hearts, and still his voice is low. Hark ! it deepens—they tremble ; it quivers - they weep ; it coaxes—they are willing ; it threatens - they shudder. It quickens, it quivers—ah ! see, he is growing diviner. He steps to the front of the platform and his voice peals forth like a trumpet, appealing, beseeching, rebuking, commanding : it trembles, and rages. and thunders in ecstacy divine. The pallid lips, now parted, pour forth a flood of fire, a many-colored tide of glowing words and thoughts. He is a vocal flame, a phosphorescent personality of melo- dious light and sound. He looks through the dust on the souls of his hearers and speaks to the spirit within. See, he holds them in the hollow of his hand ; they are angels, they are devils—as he wills."

"That might have been you," said the Old Year, "but what are you now? A dreamer. Look again. What do you see?"

"I see an author, a wizard of words and singer of beautiful songs, who dips his pen in the blood of his heart and writes immortal visions upon the brains of men. See, they crown him with laurels and he sways his pen like a sceptre, and the voice of mankind is the tongue of his fame and his throne is the heart of the world."

"That might have been you," said the Old Year. "Living and dead in glory forever, that might have been you ; but what are you now?"

"I am a tragedy," cried the Dreamer, arising to his feet. "I am a drama done behind the scenes ; I am a special creation doomed to a special destruction. My soul is like a fiery furnace molten red, and the consuming fires of genius burn my poor brain to ashes. I am the youngest brother of Shakespeare, Dante, Goethe—the divinest possibility that ever died unborn. I am a genius, I am—nothing."

"What have you left?" asked the Old Year, stealthily watching his hand.

"I have this," cried the Dreamer triumphantly, and the barrel of his revolver flashed in the light of the fire. "I always thought the world unkind until it gave me this."

(The quivering chords upon the harp of life grew harsh and tangled in a moment, and a charred breath from hell crept through the palpitating nerves, playing a tragic discord on a soul divinely sweet.)

" Fire !" cried the Old Year fiercely. " Put your gun to your eye and fire. I will bear you away in my arms."

" Hush," said the Dreamer softly, stirring the papers on the table with the point of his revolver. " The generous world which gave me—this this pretty little Christmas present— this pistol—shall have a New Year's gift from me. These are the verses I was writing when you came. We will read them softly till the clock strikes twelve, then we will pull the little trigger :

> I dreamt a dream, but ah !
> My dream is dead;
> It was a dream of things that may not be,
> It was a dream of things too sweet to see,
> And joy forever fled.

" Haste," cried the Old Year eagerly ; the hands of the clock draw near to the hour of twelve, the shadows are deepening in the west."

"So do the shadows deepen on my soul," said the Dreamer wearily. Hark !

> O dream, dead dream,
> O dream of sweetest seeming ;
> When will I dream
> My sweetest dream again?
> Dark is the night, my soul forever dreaming,
> Drifts deathward doubting
> God may be a dream.

> I am a dream
> Ghouls dreamt me in the midnight
> Lo I——

" Fire !" cried the Old Year, leaping suddenly to his feet and stretching out his withered arms to seize his willing prey. "The finger of time points to the hour of twelve, the darkest darkness thickens in the sky and I must leave the world and you must come with me."

"The darkest darkness gathers in my soul," said the Dreamer sadly, and his eye glanced dreamily down the barrel of the revolver into the dim aisles and shadow-shrouded pathways that lead from life's inferno to the dreamless valley of death.

His finger touched the trigger.

"Stop!"

A clarion voice rang through the room and a beautiful youth in garments of light, the New Year, radiant with love and joy, rose glittering on his sight, his silvery voice in music mingling with the sweet, melodious chiming of a thousand mellow bells.

"Stop. It was the mirror of the future which you saw. I will fulfil your dreams."

" I am going now," shrieked the Old Year, making a dive for the window.

"Go and be ——" cried the Dreamer, as the New Year clasped him to his heart.

For when time and a youth meet on the highways of life it is the youth who smiles.

> I heard a voice say,
> " Dreamer, dream again,
> Dream of undying hope,
> Unbended knee ;
> Dream of the laurel crown
> And victory,
> Dream, dreamer, dream again."

Genius and Patriotism.

IN the world of literature there are no nations. True genius transcends nationality. The sterility of Canadian literature to-day is due not to deficiency but to an excess of patriotism. Genius is measured by its thought and not its dialect. The true author writes not for any particular time or people, but for all peoples and all ages High above the mouldering walls which feudalism and folly have reared, there is a pure and a rarified atmosphere where thinkers meet and mingle The greatest authors have not written for the particular tribe or nation with which the accident of birth had associated them, but have penned their message for humanity. Earth itself was too small for Milton, too shallow for Dante, and too narrow for Plato. Canadians fail because they confine their work to a too limited range. The great problems of the age are not national problems. They are issues common to all men. Those who have studied the social and economic tendencies of several nations have keenly realized the fact that by a universal and inevitable snythesis the issues of national debate are broadening into issues of human impo:t The study of the novelist is human nature, not national nature. The study of the poet is human emotion, and intellect, and passion, and love, and truth, and that impartial nature which no nation can fence in. These things are common to the men of every country. The sun sends its message of light with equal impartiality to the watchers in every tribe

Patriotism is a limited altruism. It is an attribute of nationality, and must vanish with nationality But when it vanishes it will vanish not by death but by growth, or if it dies it will die as the caterpillar dies, and at its death it will take wings and soar to the lofty altitude of a golden and glorious altruism. The author who aspires to rank with the Platos and Dantes and Goethes must rise as they have risen, above all national prejudices, and speak the language of men instead of stuttering in the dialect of any peculiar tribe or nation. The grandeur of the Athenians lay in the breadth of their genius. While the citizens of other cities or nations were wrangling over local issues, these men walked in their groves and gardens discussing things eternal. The problems that occupied their minds were problems of human destiny, of human conduct and of human nature Diogenes lived in his tub and discussed the universe Aristotle, Plato, Zeno, Socrates, Epicurus are remembered to-day because they spoke of issues which every age cou'd appreciate The civil wars and broils in Florence were never deemed by Dante of sufficient impoit to distract his attention from that inspired vision which he has bequeathed to all nations and all ages.

The author who aspires to be read through the mists of the ages must write in letters of fire. The work of Canadian authors will not be less honorable in the eyes of posterity if it be found that instead of bending their eyes to the dust they turned them to the universal stars. If kings and politicians have taken upon themselves the responsibility of dividing the race into clans and nations, the author is under no compulsion to confine his thought

to the boundaries which their folly has prescribed.
Genius should not be an accessory to the crime of
nationality. The Romans chained the slave, Epictetus,
but they could not chain the philosopher. It is the
peculiar function of genius to create from its mind an
ideal universe whose only citizen is man. While the
politicians of the various nations are howling their
national anthems, or dancing a frantic war dance to
music of tradition, the poets and the philosophers stand
as old Plato stood in god-like grandeur beneath vaults
of the universe listening to the music of the spheres,
and feeling that even the world itself is too narrow a
home for that imprisoned soul whose thoughts are as
wide as the infinite and as deep as God

There are problems in art, in psychology and in
sociology which the average Canadian author never
touches on. It is idle to assert a deficiency of subjects.
There are mysteries of mind, of conduct and of nature
to be revealed. The miracle of life is yet to be ex-
plained, and the oracle of being asks from the thinkers
of this country, as it has asked of all others, an answer
to the question, "from whence and whither?" Science
and literature are closely correlated, and must soon go
on their journey to the depths hand in hand. There
are promethean depths as yet unsounded in every department of thought There are oracles still unread.
there are oceans yet unsounded, there are cities yet
unbuilt. Indeed, when we compare the things unknown
with the things we know, and see the supreme mystery
that encompasses us on every side, and how the esoteric
shrouds the exoteric like the night prevailing over the

day, we cannot but think that we are indeed upon the surface of a world and the past voices that have spoken, grand as they were, were but the lispings of an infant who some day shall rise to manhood and rend aside the veil of ether, and in no wavering voice demand an answer to the question " Why ? " Within the depths of the human mind there linger anthems which the gods might chant, songs of such subtle music that seraphs might becomingly sing them. The greatest songs are yet unsung, the wisest sayings are yet unsaid. Below the shallows seen slumber the depths invisible, and deeper than the spoken are the unspoken things Beethoven recorded the most subtle chords of music as yet revealed to man, but these only seem like the echoes, faint and feeble, of some mighty choir whose wildest and grandest melodies are yet unheard. Mozart and Handel each caught and recorded marvellous melodies, which, glorious as they are, yet seem like only the overture of an opera whose most glorious anthems are yet unsung. Spinoza, Fitche and Schelling passed through the portico of the infinite, but seemed to drop their pens before recording the things beyond Bohme, Swedenborg and Blavatsky, borne on the w ngs of a subtle mysticism, seem to have penetrated into that occult universe where the causes sit in state, and yet the light they have given us seems merely a feeble candle, which burns feebly and nervously in the midst of a dense, dark inscrutable universe. Tyndall, Crooks and Tesla, having indicated the identity of the forces in ether, have paused for a moment to tell us that they are only beginning to learn. Herbert Spen-cer, in the very inception of his philosophy, speaks of a

great "unknown." Political economy for two centuries
has been seeking a remedy for social discontent, and in
its latest utterance tells us that it has sought in vain.

Meanwhile the authors of Canada are discussing the
Fenian Raid. They tell in thrilling tones of the genesis
of the squaw and the decline and fall of the papoose.
They expatiate in glowing periods on the criminality of
Sunday street cars. The columns of an Ottawa journal
were recently occupied by a prolonged discussion between two aspiring Canadian writers on the correct and
proper spelling of the word " honour," and another great
man, " the mightiest Roman of them all," with a genius
as unique as it is rare, with a fervid patriotism that
wou'd put a Regulus to shame, and an erudition which
is unrivalled and profound, discusses the heroic achievements of the York pioneers.

Even assuming that the history of Canada were prolific of those incidents which form a fitting theme for
genius, and display in activity the more subtle qualities
of the mind, it does not follow that the Canadian author
should reject the whole of the world for a part, or confine
his studies of human nature to its manifestations in one
particular district. It must also be borne in mind that
the work of the author is not purely historical. The
most important departments of human thought are those
whose greatest development may be looked for in the
future. There are depths below depths and heights
above heights. The realms of nature are yet unread.
Even to those authors who do not aspire to deal with
the more subtle problems of the universe, or to go beyond the world in which they dwell, there is ample

material for thought and authorship in the great social and economic issues of the day. The evils of land monopoly, of unequal division of wealth, of poverty, of vice, of crime, of superstition, all form a fitting subject for the pen as well as for the voice. Ten million poverty-stricken people on this continent alone cry in agonized tones to the men of thought as well as of action to consecrate their powers to the destruction of monopoly, the organization of industry and the emancipation of the masses. Surely when the rifle is beginning to speak on the question of labour and capital, the pen should not be silent; and surely when these great and weighty issues, issues of life and death, issues of time and eternity, are awaiting a solution, the authors of Canada have not far to seek to find a sterner and worthier subject for their genius than the decline of the bison, or the beauty of Muskoka lakes.

A nation is made honourable by the honour of its men, and its greatness is measured by the capacities of its people. Had the authors of Athens never arisen above the barriers of nationality, Athens would be forgotten to-day. If the authors of Canada content themselves with the discussion of local issues, obscurity will be their reward. It behooves them to turn their eyes from the shallows to the depths, to recognize the fact that national divisions in no sense represent mental distinctions, and to lend that genius which they possess in no less degree than any other people or era to the elucidation of those profound problems of race and intellect and society which form the common heritage of every people. Let it be said of this Canada of ours that it

produced men whose minds were broad, whose aspira
tions were lofty, and who, standing on this spot of Mother
Earth, looked higher than the walls that men have built
and saw inspired visions in the skies.   Let it be said
that, wide as their country is, their minds are wider, that
while Canadians in name they are god-like in nature, and
are elevated by the power of an aspiration which nation
ality can never cripple and tradition can never stain.

But if, on the other hand, the authors of this country
continue to cower behind the walls of nationality, to
tune their souls to the harmonies of the party machine,
and to mumble in the dialect of a tribe instead of speaking the language of humanity, I cannot but think it
altogether fitting and proper that their reward should be
proportioned to their ambition, and their work be paid
for in a coin as visionary as the feudal phantoms they
adore.

Apollo and Tomkins.

APOLLO—It makes me weary—it makes me exceedingly weary to read about other fellows doing the great thing while we poor modern devils are doomed by the asinine mediocrity of the age to live like cows in stalls and chew the cud of civilization. Men don't live nowadays; they merely exist; they are machines, they are moles, they are worms. The world is worn out, aged and sear; the blood runs cold, the pulse beats slow, the wine of life is sour, the flowers of joy are withered, the lights burn low. Life is a failure.

TOMKINS—Nonsense. What do you know about life?—a foolish boy barely out of his teens! This is the most highly civilized epoch in the history of the world.

APOLLO—And what is civilization but a coffin where the ancient joys lie buried? One splendid moment of wild barbaric joy was worth a century of this. Give me the ancient ecstasy—when the world was savage and free and the battle of life was fought in a garden of flowers—bright skies, bright eyes, bright hopes, red wine, red lips, red blood, great hearts, great hopes, great hates, the lust for life, the battle joy.

TOMKINS—Heroes are fools. They were too primitive to be practical. If you get three meals a day you needn't complain. Look after number one. If you don't skin the other fellow he'll skin you. Make a dive for the dough whenever you see it. Life ain't so bad if

you've got the stuff   The rich man is always fash·on-
able.   Cash will open any door in Toronto or elsewhere.
Who made society influential and polite?

APOLLO—No one made it polite, but someone called
it polite, and what a sweet exchange you offer for the
deep joys of old.   You spend your life making cash to
open the door of joy, and when the cash is made your
life is gone.   You stand old and tired before the door of
society with a golden key in your hand.   You open it
and find—a garden of roses?   No, but a select company
of silly females and rattle-brained, simpering men—a
hierarchy of mediocrities, where it is positively unfashionable to be intelligent, and criminal to be clever.
Did you ever hear an original remark in a drawing-
room?

TOMKINS—Not often, but then I have seldom met you
out, you know.   I have, however, seen some clever men
—not too clever, you know—just clever.

APOLLO—The men of to-day have milk in their veins
instead of blood.

TOMKINS—Milk!   What of our football p'ayers, our
hockey——

APOLLO—Ye gods!   How Achilles would have smiled
to see the sons of an imperial race, descendants of the
men whose fathers conquered nations and wrote immortal epics, chasing a dirty piece of pigskin around the field
or floundering like silly schoolboys on the ice!   What
an intellectual effort it requires to be a civilized young
man!

TOMKINS—I am appalled at your superiority.   We have
some students, however, in the town—some colleges.

APOLLO—Where the minds of boys are stuffed with threadbare, worn-out thoughts of other men ; where the flower of youth is wasted in the charnel atmosphere of lecture-rooms and library ; their eyes grow dim, the roses fade from their cheeks, their brows grow wrinkled. They bring knowledge away from college and leave their youth behind. I love a man as Nature made him, before the chains of civilization were laid upon him to cripple and deform. I love him in all his primitive simplicity — barbaric, beautiful and free—the brother of the roses, the lily and the dew, the comrade of the stars, alive and thrilling with creative music—the music of the storm.

TOMKINS—Oh, give us a rest ! I'm hungry ! I'm going home ! I want some grub !

Toronto, Feb., '97.

The Last Patient.

HE threw himself into a chair and covered his face with his hands. The long winter's drive was over at last, but the cold of the night was still in his veins and his brain felt heavy and numb.

"I have overdone it," he muttered wearily. "There is a limit to nature's endurance. I have passed the limit to-night."

It had been a terrible journey—twenty miles through the heavy snow on the coldest of winter nights. Even now in the quiet of his study and before the blaze of the fire he could feel the sting of the frost upon his face and hear the surge of the remorseless wind as it drove the pitiless hail on his brow. The strain had been too great —too great for a frame already weakened and emaciated by a too close attendance to duty. Since the fever epidemic had entered the neighborhood and carried off two of his fellow physicians among its victims, the burden of his duty had been greatly increased. By day and night, with unremitting care, he had gone upon his rounds and faced the common enemy in a hundred different homes. His life for the last few weeks had been one long succession of visits varied only by occasional brief intervals of rest. Last night he had known no sleep, and this day, though feeling strangely sick, he had pursued the round of his visits and had only now returned from a drive of twenty miles to sink in utter exhaustion into his easy-chair.

"I have got it—the fever," he muttered, staring dizzily at the fire.

And in the quiet of the study he could hear the noisy throbbing of his heart beating tumultuously, while the blood coursed madly through his veins and he felt a weight like lead upon his brain. With aching eyes and mind distraught with care, he gazed unsteadily forward into the fire and seemed to see death in the flames. He longed for rest but could not rest; sleep, and he could not sleep, for there was anarchy in his brain and his heart was freighted with fire.

"Sooner or later," he murmured feebly. "Just as well soon as late."

No, he had little to lose by death. All that he loved he had lost a little while before and what remained was hardly worth possessing. He shuddered as he looked around, oppressed by his isolation from the world and by the utter loneliness and hopelessness of life. He thought of other scenes and days—other and sweeter scenes—other and happier days, and one death-dealing day—the darkest day of all, when his heart had been broken in twain, and the light of his life had gone out. She had been very cruel. It was that which led to this—he had nothing to live for now.

His patients, yes, his patients—he should certainly live for them—see their faces float before him—faces living and dead. Fevered faces, pallid faces—they floated before him in the twilight—faces of strong men in agony, and women and little children—little, little children, how they circled around him, and stared at him with cold, unpitying eyes, and opened pallid lips to murmur :

" Physician, heal thyself."

With a mocking laugh he leaped to his feet, half waking, half asleep, till the noise of his laughter recalled his scattered senses and startled him to a consciousness of his surroundings.   His professional instincts and his professional pride revolted at his previous hesitance. He staggered to his feet and mixed a glass of medicine, drank it, and sank back in his chair.   "I must have sleep," he muttered.   "I am weak—weak.   Another night like the last and I am finished.   I cannot go out to night though the devil himself should call.   I will not go out to-night."

" Tinkle—tinkle—tinkle."

It was the bell of the telephone vibrating suddenly on the silence.

With a smothered curse the doctor sprang to his feet, then sank back again in his chair.

" Let it ring and be ——," he muttered.   " I will not go out to night."

" Tinkle—tinkle—tinkle."

Imperious and petulant the bell rang through the house, calling him to duty.

"I dare not," he muttered weakly.   "I must have rest to-night."

" Tinkle—tinkle—tinkle."

Who could it be?   Which of his patients was it? Their faces flitted before him, one by one, and he wondered which it could be who summoned him now so impressively in the midnight to risk his life for theirs.

His heart was stirred to bitter indignation and revolt at the persistent cruelty of the bell.

"Tinkle—tinkle—tinkle."

With a smothered curse he jumped to his feet and eagerly strode to the telephone.

"Who is it?" he shouted angrily. "What do you want? Who is it?"

And then it was that there came suddenly to his ear, borne with swift, electric impulse along the throbbing wire, a word—a name which stirred him like a trumpet and sent the hot blood rushing through his veins in an ecstasy of pleasure—and of pain.

"Adele."

"Adele!" he echoed. "You?"

"Yes. Come—come quickly."

"I will come—yes, quickly," he answered rapidly, every nerve in his body thrilling at this supreme appeal. She was ill—the light of his life, the light of the world—she was ill. He forgot the cruel past. The tube of the telephone dropped from his hand and he turned towards the door.

.   .   .   .

The patient lay upon his bed in the gray house on the hill and watched with restless eye the figure of a woman who sat in a chair by the window of the bedroom and looked out into the night. The face of the patient, flushed with fear, was also drawn in pain. There was a frown upon his brow and a strange, bitter passion lurking in his eyes, not born of physical disease, but seeming of the symptom of some other fever—some fever older and more malignant—which doctors could not cure. The source of his mental disquietude was obviously the woman at the window, from whom his eyes, steadily staring forward, were never removed for a moment.

" You telephoned for a doctor, Adele," he murmured hoarsely.   " Who ? "

" Martyn."

" Why Martyn ? " he queried jealously.   " Why Martyn, I say ? "

" The other two are dead," she said resentfully.   " He is the only one available."

" Then I must have him or die.   It is Martyn or death, eh ? " groaned the patient, turning restlessly on his pillow.

" Yes," she answered wearily.

" Or Martyn and death," muttered the patient viciously beneath his breath, as he relapsed again into silence.

She looked out into the darkness of the night and wondered if he would come. It seemed so long ago since she had seen him, so long ago since they had met and parted, hoping never to meet again. So long ago it seemed since on that night of nights in the perfumed conservatory—surrounded by flowers in full bloom, by roses, and hyacinths, and violets, and thorns—he had knelt and sobbed at her feet, asking in vain the love she gave to that poor thing on the bed—to him and his gold. Yes, it seemed very long ago since she had answered " No " and sent him forth from her presence a broken-hearted man, vowing never to see her again—and now would he come ?

"He thinks it is me," she murmured, and in the silence of the night the thought was very sweet.

A sound of a step in the distance drawing nearer and nearer—now it was at the door. She must meet him and tell him the truth. She left the window and passed to the parlor below, and glancing at a mirror on her way shuddered to see the paleness of her face. They met in the parlor. He started back in surprise. "Adele," he cried. "You——"

"Yes, I."

"I thought——"

"——I was ill."

"You said——"

"To come."

"Thank God," he cried impulsively, "it is not you—thank God." As he spoke he staggered slightly. The reaction had been too great. He sank in a chair feeling faint. She glanced at him anxiously. He had changed very little with time, and his eyes were still filled with the same wonderful love that had glanced in them on the night when she set her little foot upon his heart.

He sat for a moment in silence, striving to grasp the situation, then suddenly raised his head.

"Not you," he said. "Then who?"

"Henry."

"Who?"

"Henry."

He sprang to his feet with an oath. There was a flush of righteous anger on his face.

"Woman, woman, are you mad, or pitiless as hate to send for me—for him?"

His heart was filled to bursting with bitter indignation and despair, at this, her crowning cruelty. He walked towards the door.

" Arthur."

When could he resist that voice ? He paused at the doorway.

" Well ?"

" See him or—he will die."

" Let him die and be——. Ah, he will die ! "

The full meaning of the words flashed suddenly upon him then, breaking in a flood of joy upon his heart and opening up new vistas and possibilities to his mind.

" He will die," he muttered. " And then, Adele, and then——"

She shuddered and turned away, but her lips at least were true.

"Save him," she whispered feebly, and led the way upstairs.

The patient lay upon his bed and heard with hungry ears the voices down below. He cursed the God that made him helpless and placed him at the mercy of his rival. "He can save me. He can kill me," he muttered feverishly. " Which will she tell him to do ? " With clenched hands and panting breath he lay upon his bed and awaited the coming of his fate.

Now there were steps on the stairs. He counted them one by one. They paused. Hark to the whispers outside the door :

"Save him."

" Adele, you ask too much."

The door was opened softly, and they entered the

room together. The doctor walked to the side of the bed with a step unsteady and slow, and sank in a chair by the side of his patient. He was feeling strangely ill, and as the prospect of another sleepless night loomed up before him he seemed to see beyond it the shadow of the valley of death.

" Leave us," he said to the woman. " I will watch by his side to-night."

She shuddered and left the room.

.   .   .   .

That night a devil dark as night and cruel as fate rose up from the depths of hell and hovered above the gray house on the hlll, and, even as he hovered, preparing to descend, lo ! the gates of heaven flew open wide and an angel bright as light and fair as day swept downwards and wrestled with the devil above the gray house on the hill.

.   .   .   .

And when she entered the room in the morning the patient lay upon his bed and slept the sleep of health, with smiles upon his lips, and by his side the doctor knelt, his dead white hand upon the living pulse—and slept the sleep that knows no waking.

Two Historic Costumes.

"IT might have been for you, sir," said the valet, "it fits so well."

"It does, indeed," answered O'Grady carelessly; "I seem to have worn it before."

"Impossible, sir," said the valet; "it's a hundred—two hundred years old——"

"Impossible, of course," said O'Grady impatiently, "and yet it seems——"

"Will you not look in the mirror, sir?" said the servant enthusiastically. "Ah, what a beautiful fit!"

"One moment," said the purchaser as he buckled the belt to his side and drew the sword from its sheath, "but what is this on the sword? The steel is soiled—"

"It is blood, sir," answered the valet proudly. "A stain, sir—a stain of blood; the blood of some noble lord. The sword is old; it has seen service, sir."

"And so has the suit," said O'Grady ruefully; "but my purse has seen service, too, and we must adapt the one to the other. Oh, these historic balls!"

"The suit has been used but little," answered the valet eagerly. "One owner was killed in a duel a few nights after he bought it. There was a quarrel at the ball, and then the duel; but the suit is as good as new—all but that place that is stitched—there where the sword went through."

He placed his fingers on a little spot cleverly stitched and just above the heart, but O'Grady started suddenly back.

" Don't touch me," he cr'ed, " It pains."

The valet looked at him wonderingly, then smiled in sudden understanding of the situation.

" Imagination," he said. " I have met with it before in noble gentlemen who say that when they put on these suits they seem to assume the characters of their owners.

" Assume—or resume," muttered O'Grady, thought-fully glancing at the cavalier who, attired in the costume of a courtier of Louis XIV., confronted him in the mirror. It was a very different costume from what he had worn all day, and yet it seemed very familiar. It might have been his daily dress, so perfectly natural did it seem.

" *Mon dieu !* how becoming it is," cried the valet enthusiastically, echoing his thoughts. " It might have been made for you, sir."

" Perhaps it was," said O'Grady, half smiling at the conceit. " Who did you say was the owner?"

" The Count de Lavat, sir," answered the servant, "a courtier of Louis XIV., stationed for a time at Quebec, where he was killed in a duel by le Viscount de Grassi——"

" Lavat—de Grassi," muttered O'Grady under his breath. " How familiar—how familiar."

" *Mon dieu !* what ails you, sir ? " cried the valet, alarmed at the change in the voice of O'Grady, who had started suddenly back with his hand upon his sword.

" I remember, ah, I remember," answered his master wildly. " It all comes back to me now. I have lived before to-day—this sword—this suit—Violette and de Grassi—where is he?''

"Eh, sir, I do not know," said the servant, "but his suit is gone to the ball. A gentleman called Wilkins purchased it, and just like you he say—when he look in the glass he say, 'My God, where is Lavat?'"

"Ah, traitor, I will find you," cried O'Grady fiercely, and with an angry scowl he hastened away to the Armories.

CHAP. II.　AT THE BALL.

"Lavat."

"De Grassi."

In the middle of the Armories two courtiers of Louis XIV. confronted each other fiercely.

"You killed me in a duel a hundred years ago," hissed Lavat fiercely.

"I am delighted to hear it," answered De Grassi haughtily; "and what about it, sir?"

"Where is Violette?"

"Dear me! Are you after her still?" answered the other insolently. "O these historic balls!"

"She comes," cried the other wildly, as a beautiful figure drew near.

"Violette!" they cried simultaneously.

"De Lavat—De Grassi," she muttered. "(What a nuisance.) This is like old times, is it not?"

"I love you!" cried Lavat.

"What! must I kill you again?" shrieked De Grassi.

"Will you do me a service?" she asked sweetly.

The cavaliers fell on their knees.

"Wander away to the Osgoode Hall grounds and kill each other again," she answered dreamily. "I have but one dance and will give it to the survivor."

CHAPTER III. THE DUEL.

The moon shone brightly in the winter sky and cast her pale and spectral beams on the grounds of Osgoode Hall. A couple of courtiers in the costume of the time of Louis XIV., accompanied by their seconds, confronted each other in the snow, prepared to engage in mortal combat.

"Villain!" hissed De Grassi, as he threw his hat on the ground.

"Traitor!" shrieked Lavat, as he drew his sword from its sheath.

One by one they removed their coats and vests to ease them while at combat, and as they laid the historic costumes on the ground the character of the courtier vanished with them, and a sudden recollection brought to light the real identity of the warriors.

"Hallo, O'Grady!" cried Wilkins.

"Is that you, Wilkins?" cried O'Grady.

Oh, these historic balls!

An Exile from Erin.

(*T. D'Arcy McGee.*)

It is now nearly thirty years since the bullet of Whalen removed from the field of public affairs in Canada one of the most brilliant and fascinating figures that has ever appeared in the arena of Canadian politics. "An Exile from Erin" he came to our shores and by the witchery of art and charm of resistless eloquence won for himself an enduring regard in the affections of his chosen countrymen. Driven by an adverse fate from the shores of Old Ireland, he drifted first to America, then to Canadian soil, and found in the legislature of the nebulous nation a fitting field for the exercise of his gifts. At the parturition period of this country's history he threw into the scale of its political forces the weight of his wisdom and his wit, and lived to see the warring forces reconciled, and class and creed and races and religions bound and blent together in the great consummation of Confederation. Then, in the prime of life, with his foot implanted on the threshold of the new-born nation, and his eloquent mind glowing with visions of future greatness in the councils of the vast Dominion, the shadow of the past fell heavily upon him, and the cruel hand of Fenianism snatched him from the service of his country, amidst whose enlightened councils and liberal institutions he had learned the lesson of toleration and loyalty.

The secret of the death and conduct of McGee must be right in the history of his early life. His present

was perpetually haunted by his past and the shadow of
an early error hung heavily over the vista of a life made
radiant by many kindly deeds.

It was a dark day in Dublin, where many days are
dark, when the spirit of O'Connell passed away, freeing
the eager agitators of the " Young Ireland " faction from
the last restraint to their fatal ambition to realize visions
by violence. Already the agitation for the repeal of the
Union initiated by the great tribune had gone farther
than his wildest dreams had ever ventured, and led by
famine and strengthened by suffering, had hovered dan-
gerously near the perilous ridge of revolution. The
flames his eloquence had kindled fed on the hopes his
heart had cherished and the generation which echoed
his denunciations to Britain rejected his counsels of
peace.

The year 1848, which witnessed the occurrence of the
rebellion which necessitated the departure of McGee
from Ireland was then prolific of great events, not only in
Ireland, but in almost every country in Europe.
Throughout the whole of the Continent the smouldering spirit of revolution, so long subdued and crushed, at
last burst forth with a tragic intensity which shook
every throne in Europe. In France the barricades were
erected and the red lines of flame sweeping down the
bloody aisles of the boulevards emancipated the country
from the monarchy. In Italy the heroic followers of Mazzini and Garibaldi had reaped the fruits of innumerable
conspiracies and waged their gallant war for freedom
with great, but short-lived success. In Hungary the
genius of Kossuth had kindled the souls of the Magyars

and the genius of liberty flashed fitfully forth from the ill-fated bayonets of Gorgey. In the German states the demand for constitutional freedom was fiercely echoed by millions of turbulent voices, and even in Russia the serf was shaking his chains. And was it to be expected that Ireland, restless, emotional, impatient, would remain silent in the midst of this universal turmoil, particularly when the voice of the most eloquent orators had combined with the exactions of the landlords, and the energy of their bailiffs to convince her peasantry that they were the most injured people in the world? The agitation for the repeal of the Union inaugurated by O'Connell had, even before he died, passed far beyond his control, and fanned by the fiery eloquence of a rising generation of brilliant men, had developed into an impassioned agitation bordering very closely on revolution for the establishment of an independent Irish nation. And now the voice of the agitator and the zeal of the bailiff had found a terrible auxiliary in the great famine, which, sweeping over the country, completed the misery of the people and reduced the unfortunate peasants to a condition of abject destitution and poverty.

At this time D'Arcy McGee, as editor of *The Dublin Nation*, was one of the most conspicuous of that brilliant band of Irish journalists who voiced the sentiments of the Young Ireland party, and vigorously incited the people to rise and emancipate themselves from British rule. They were no Home Rulers, but Nationalists out and out, and demanded nothing less than the complete independence of Ireland. They pointed with passionate indignation to the poverty of the people, to the

exactions of the landlords, to the starvation of the peasantry, to the destitution of the country, and recklessly
declared that all these had been caused by British rule,.
and would be cured by Irish independence. They
painted with a glowing and poetic eloquence the future
of an Irish nation with all her people rich and happy,
sans landlords, sans bailiffs, sans famine, sans poverty,
and the green flag over all. And the poor peasantry,
hungry and ragged, and driven to desperation by the
terrible famine, but ever hopeful, ever imaginative, and
ever responsive to the voice of eloquence, prepared to
arm themselves for the impending struggle, and with
rusty muskets in their ragged arms go forth to fight for
Ireland under the leadership of the valiant Dublin journalists. There is something strangely pathetic in the cre-
dulity of these people, who have so often failed but never
faltered, and knowing every mood but despair, cower
among their wretched huts and cherish a hope not born
of idle dreams that all will yet be well. The sun forever sinking has never set on Ireland, and the genius of
her people is seen forever shining in the twinkle of an
eye, the smile upon their lips and the unquenchable
kindness of their large and loving hearts. The year 1848
found them, as usual, at the disposal of the loudest agitators, poor but patriotic, always willing, but seldom ready,
ever brave and ever blind, always determined and always
deluded, and never more completely destined to make
their periodic and proverbial plunge from the sublime to
the ridiculous.

As the year advanced the preparations for an uprising
became more extensive and more violent. The success

of the revolutionists in France greatly encouraged the
agitators in Dublin and sealed their determination to
make an early and desperate attempt to emancipate Ireland.   The capital became a focus of conspiracy, where
in secret council leaders of the movement met daily and
nightly, arranging and completing their plans for the
uprising.   There were seen the most daring spirits of
the land, and with them agents from America, and
emissaries from Europe, and there, too, as the event
proved, in large numbers, was the inevitable informer.
It is a difficult thing for an Irishman to keep a secret,
and with all deference to the Clan-na-Gael we very
humbly submit that the Irish were not originally intended by nature to play the role of conspirators.   Certain
it is that all the plans of the would-be revolutionists in
1848 were speedily divulged to the British Government,
and there can be little doubt that over in London the
movement was watched with perhaps as much amuse-
ment as alarm.   And yet it was, in its inception at
least, perhaps the most serious attempt that had been
made in Ireland for a century to throw off British rule.
Never had the time been more favorable.   O'Connell
had been sowing the seeds of discontent for thirty years
before.   The great famine had made the people desperate, the success of the revolutionists in Europe had
inspired them with hope, and the leaders of the movement in Dublin, young and rash as they were, were yet
men of exceptional ability and sincerity, and well dowered with eloquence, enthusiasm, and energy.   Into
this great movement D'Arcy McGee threw himself with
all the energy of his impulsive nature, and of all the

fierce denunciations of British rule his were, perhaps, the most passionate, the most reckless, and the most eloquent. He waved the green banner frantically in the air, and told in glowing language of the time when it would float in glory over a great Irish nation and be the pride and inspiration of the innumerable poets and heroes, orators and philosophers of Erin.

The result of this uprising of 1848 is too familiar to require repetition here, and it is sufficient to say that when the short struggle was over the leaders, who but a short time before had been the idols of their country-men, were either lying in a felon's jail or hiding from the officers of justice. In discussing this rebellion at a later period in America, McGee fiercely denounced the priests as the cause of the failure, declaring that they had compelled the people to abstain from action at the critical moment of the contest. Whatever the causes of the failure of the attempt may have been the results were most disastrous to its promoters. McGee himself after lying in concealment managed to escape to the United States disguised as a priest. In New York he was eagerly welcomed by many of his sympathizers, and continued in the Irish-American journals as well as on the lecture platforms his bitter and virulent attacks on English rule in Ireland. He also fell foul of the Church, and attacked the priests for their share in the rebellion. This difficulty, which caused much loss to McGee both in the prestige he enjoyed among his Catholic countrymen and in the financial support of his paper, was finally adjusted, and he became reconciled to the Church, and remained a Catholic to his death.

With time and study his anti-British sentiments became
considerably moderated and his intellectual horizon
grew wider. He lectured with great eloquence in
American cities on a large variety of subjects, and finally,
in response to an earnest invitation from the Irish
colony in Montreal, decided to make his future resi-
dence in Canada.

In considering the character of McGee at this period
there can be little doubt that he would be best described
as a demagogue. The bitter experiences of political
perfidy and of harsh realities of life which he had
undergone in Ireland and America, had embittered his
views of human nature. The period of disillusion had
arrived. The sanguine dreams of youth had been too
rudely shattered to revive. His confidence in human
nature was shaken, he had seen it sink so low. He was
driven from the country of his birth, and forced
to wander a stranger in a strange land and battle
sternly for a living far away from those early associa-
tions, which perhaps alone possessed the power to call
forth the highest qualities of his nature. His castles in
the air had all been rudely shattered. He had little interest in the political issues of the new lands, and his
one apparent object at this time was to utilize his great
talents for the advancement of his personal interests.

Such was D'Arcy McGee at the time of his advent
in Canadian politics. And in his character as it then
was, uncertain and aimless, is the key to his somewhat
eccentric political attitude or series of attitudes when he
entered the Legislature. There for a time his remarkable abilities ran riot, always manifest but rarely directed

to the achievement of any permanent or enduring end,
and generally dissipated in the service of some tempor-
ary political exigency.

As time advanced, however, and his great oratorical
powers, though not directed to any definite end, made
him one of the most conspicuous, powerful politicians
of the country. McGee began to acquire a genuine and
permanent interest in those new political issues which
formerly he had used as playthings. The ambition so
rudely shattered in Ireland revived in his new sphere,
and he determined to fashion for himself a new career
in Canada. He studied with much interest the short
but romantic his'ory of the new land, and his poetical
mind found abundant inspiration in the splendid scenery
and legendary lore of Quebec and the neighboring
Provinces. He loved to dwell on the times when the
stately courtiers of Louis XIV. sailed over the sea to
found a new and freer France beside the great St. Law-
rence. He liked to dwell on the heroic achievements
of Cartier, La Salle, Frontenac, and Champlain, and the
heroic struggles of the red men to maintain the land
against the strangers. He liked to tell of the rivalry of
Saxon and Celt, of the heroism of our pioneers, and the
journeys of the priests, and the planting of the cross in
the wilderness. And he could paint in winning words
a perfect picture of the great linked lakes so vast and
misty, waiting in the rustling forest for the commerce of
the centuries, or tell of the broad pulsating rivers, the
daring rugged mountains, the quiet fertile valleys and
the forests of pine and fir and maple, and the slumbering wealth of gold and silver and coal—all waiting for

the wonderful days to be. With magical eloquence he would tell of chateau and hut and wigwam, seigneur and chieftain and settler, the ring of the axe, the crack of the rifle, the war cry of Iroquois, the whisper of the winds, the rustle of the forest, the birch canoe gently gliding down the musical running waters, the low cabin in the forest, the settler over his fireside, the howl of the wolf in the distance, the harsh shriek from the forest, the sudden alarm, the crack of the trusty rifle, the brand of fire and burning hut, the death of torture, the requiem of the winds—the silence. All the mystery and misery, all the sunshine and sorrow, and all the danger and the daring, all the turmoil and the triumph, and in it all and over all triumphant, he would tell of the conquering Celt and Saxon, rulers of men and builders of nations, and so he spoke with music of thought and word and eye, music of soul and sense and sight, and music of memory, mirth, and myth.

And thus the brilliant exile learned to love the land he lived in, and his rich imagination going backward to the era of conflict returned to see the divergent forces reconciled, converging into the frame and form and pattern and proportion of a majestic nation; and with this brightest picture in his mind and on his lips, D'Arcy Mc-Gee became the orator of Confederation. In the few years immediately preceding his death his mind grew broader and his vision keener, and the reckless politician developed into a statesman capable of handling with weight and dignity the large and fundamental problems involved in the constitutional evolution of a nation. On the Irish question his views had also changed very considerably, and he signed his own death warrant by repudiating his former extreme opinions, and advocating the continued union of Great Britain and Ireland. But though he could repudiate his opinions he could never repudiate his past. The memory of the past haunted him perpetually. It followed him over the waste of waters, ever abiding with him, stealthily, silently tracking him to his doom. He had advanced and grown with years, but there were those of his countrymen who had neither advanced nor grown, but standing in the shadow of ignorance viewed with the bitterest resentment his growing fealty to Britain. They could not follow him as he ascended, but only cowering in the darkness decreed that he must die. His past destroyed him, snatching him with felon's hand from the future that so anxiously awaited his coming. And yet he was never false to Ireland. His only treason was that transcendent treason which marks the movement of an expanding intellect repudiating ancient error to worship with heroic heresy at the altar of a new-born truth. A time there had been when he had served his country " not wisely but too well," and a later time there was when he served her both well and wisely.

Never was the wayward Irish exile so supremely great as in that last pathetic struggle to rise above the darkness of the past, when, with full knowledge of the deadly risk he ran, he told the honest truth to Ireland. Nor will the people of Canada, to which he gave the flower of his days, begrudge that in his dying hours his mind went back to that dear Ireland which for loving he had lost. The green grass grows on Irish soil, and

loving eyes turn backward to the land on whose gray
hills and humble homes the sunlight of perpetual patriotism is seen forever shining, and who can send her
sons beyond the farthest seas, and yet retain them to the
very last.   The debt we owe to Ireland for McGee this
country has striven to repay with Blake.   Over the
same broad sea where fifty years ago the Irish lad came
sailing to fame and fortune now there has gone back to
Irish soil a soldier well equipped with nature's choicest
weapons and her wit ; and let us hope that they who
hear his voice and bow before the magic of his mind will
feel some portion of that rare delight which thrilled Canadian hearts when the silvery voice of the " Exile from
Erin " rang through our council halls.

An Ode to a Book.

Strange cradle where the master-mind
  Has laid his child to rest,
Within whose limits, firm, defined
  A mind has been compressed ;
    And in whose pages, calm and clear,
    Great thoughts in formal shapes appear.

What art thou, that canst thus retain
  In limits so defined,
The thoughts that stormed and raged and seethed
  In the creative mind?
    And from the vortex of the soul,
    Into thy ready mould did roll.

Hast thou no tale, except the tale
  Thy pages here unfold ;
No traces of the tempest wild,
  That in the mind had rolled ;
    Nor of the strife of warring thought,
    Amidst whose chaos thou wert wrought ?

Hast thou no mention of the thought
  That wrestled with the thought you give ;
Or of the awful carnage wrought,
  Before the living thought could live ?
    How from the soul's chaotic world,
    A Lucifer was hurled ?

O ! wondrous book, that thus canst hold,
  Within the compass of thy pages ;
Thoughts that like living tempest rolled,
  And echoed down the wondering ages,
    Dreams that for other worlds have striven,
    And hopes that wandered near to heaven.

But where, ah ! where is he—the thinker,
  The mind that shed thy fruitful germs ;
And what art thou that hast a being,
  While he that made thee feeds the worms,
    And while his bones in earth are lying,
    Thou still art here—exempt from dying ?

And every eye that views thy pages,
  And gazes wondering on thy story,
Will lose its light—while other ages
  Are bringing tribute to thy glory.
    The sons of men are laid to rest,
    While thou eternally art blessed.

And what was that which gave thee power
  To sail unsinking on the sea ?
Whose was the brain that toiled an hour
  To win eternity for thee ?
    That faded when it gave thee birth,
    And mingled with its mother earth.

    *   *   *   *   *   *

He lived in times when minds were shrouded,
  But saw the light, and in it wrought ;

And after hours, perplexed and clouded,
  Brought forth a thought,
    And tremblingly to thee consigned
    The sacred treasure of his mind,
    Bidding thee give it to mankind.

He lived to see his work derided,
  And ignorance smote him with a curse ;
But grandly rising he defied it,
  Then called his hearse,
    And left thy calm and tear stained pages
    To bear his greeting to the ages.

The flame he kindled now is burning,
  The world grows happier in its light,
And opening minds are daily learning
  To bless the champion of the night.
    A hundred statues mark his glory,
    A thousand voices tell his fame,
    The friends of freedom rush to battle,
    And win their battle in his name.

* * * * * *

And thou the offspring of his sorrow,
  Faint shadow of the master-mind,
Thou dost behold the golden morrow ;
  But he—Ah ! he is blind,
    And to the world's triumphant choral,
    The worm is echoing back a moral.

At the Point.

"How close we are to tragedy," she said, nervously glancing at the dark waters by the edge of the canoe.

" How close indeed," he muttered, remembering he sat by a woman.

The music of the band at Hanlan's came softly floating over the waters, gently mingling with the murmur of the waves, and, vaguely outlined in the distance, the voyagers could see a ghostly promenade of shadows passing slowly to and fro upon the shore. The sound of music, softened and mellowed by the distance, throbbed upon the air, blending in sweet, melodious unison with the ripple of waves and the murmur of passing voices, till the waters far beneath them throbbed with great harmonies and little melodies floated on invisible wings about the boat.

" Suppose I fell overboard, would you save me ?" she asked her companion, anticipating the conventional " certainly," but Trevor was silent, though her eyes were fixed on him.

" You do not answer," she muttered petulantly.

" Why should I ?" he answered carelessly. " The question is superfluous."

There was a silence again in the boat, while she strove to grasp his meaning unavailingly, but with the usual vanity of woman placed a flattering interpretation on his remark and waited for another.

They were not alone on the waters. Other boats passed softly to and fro upon the surface of the waves, noiselessly in and out of the shadows, but yet their vocal isolation was complete, and this was an ideal occasion for the anticipated proposal. Surely this was the time of times for the word of words to be said; but her beauty had a rival in the night, and the soul of the thinker in cosmic communion with the spirit of nature around was becoming splendidly oblivious of the human. And yet she must break this silence.

"It is a fine night," she said emphatically, as though she were describing a pudding.

He looked at her wonderingly, and his poet's eyes were filled with startled horror and a sense of vague repulsion thrilled his soul.

"Surely the occasion is worthy of a more original remark than that," he said impatiently, and his spirit, stirred profoundly by the beauty of the night and moved in depths she could not dream of, revolted at the inadequacy of the phrase.

"Can it be that you are only ordinary?" he said.

"Why do you call me ordinary?" she asked in wonder and dimly conscious that she said a word which made the other word impossible.

"I call you ordinary because you have profaned the splendid silence of this night by a commonplace remark," he said savagely, turning the boat to the shore with a sense of bitter disillusion.

"Perhaps you could suggest a remark equal to the occasion," she said sneeringly.

A splendid sentence trembled on his lips ready to

blossom in speech and mingle with the music of the
night and take its place in that vague orchestra of elemental sound and light which thrilled the air around.
His lips were opened but he suddenly paused. "She is
only a woman" he thought, and turned the boat to the
shore.

"He is a poet," she shuddered, and asked, "Is this
the point?"

"It is Hanlan's Point," he answered. "The other
point you missed."

Impressions of Rossetti.

A MONG the list of eminent decadents in whose work that very original critic, Max Nordau, has discovered symptoms of degeneration is Dante Gabriel Rossetti. The poet has accordingly been relegated by this amiable critic to that long list of the illustrious insane in which he has included so many of the most eminent writers of the day, and among them, of course, that school of literary impressionists with whose work the verse of Rossetti bears so delicate and subtle an affinity. It will be some consolation to the admirers of the poet to reflect that the harsh opinion of Nordau is entirely at variance with the verdict of that higher and rational school of criticism which, with hardly a dissenting voice, has assigned to this poet a foremost place among that exalted band of minstrels whose lofty mission it has been to find a rhythmic voice for those sublimer harmonies which move the spirit of man to alternate smiles and tears. The critics have been very kind to Rossetti, perhaps because he was kind to the critics. He set before them a dainty dish, which even the most fastidious intellectual epicure could hardly fail to relish ; and it would be a difficult thing indeed to find a flaw in any one of those beautiful sonnets which he wrought with such exquisite care, in which the soul of music seems to slumber, and which seem not only poetry, but the very essence of poetry.

The limitations of Rossetti are more obvious than his

defects. His work is not characterized by that universal sympathy, that cosmic breadth and depth of thought,
and great imaginative power which is generally conceived to be the visible stamp and seal of the highest
form of genius. There are here no vast and primitive
emotions, no turbulent upheavals of the depths, none
of that great titanic wrath and rapture, those tragic
heights and depths of pain and passion which thrill us
with sudden and tempestuous emotion in the poets and
prophets of old. There is none of the heroic grandeur
of Homer, the sublime passion of Æschylus, the flame-
clad imaginings of Dante, the prophetic ecstasy of
Isaiah. We do not find these things in the work of
Rossetti. His is essentially the poetry of a highly civilized epoch, subtle, sensitive, and refined. Passion indeed there is, indeed as terrible and as intense as ever
rent the stormy heart of Prometheus, or moved the
stony eyes of Loke to tears. But this emotion wears
a veil, and tears its pallid face away, utters no heaven-
rending cry of agony, but in a whisper hushed and sibi-
lant, voices a grief as cruel as death or night. Under
the influence of the great emotions the voice sinks to
a whisper. The deepest grief is not the most audible.
In this age of self-repression passion cowers behind the
prison bars of sense, and Will, the warder, holds the
lock and key. Our sorrow is subdued. Our grief is
not the grief of angry gods, but the deep and inexpres-
sible anguish of a silent, inexplicable sphinx.

And yet though his range is limited, and his sympathies are far from universal, I sometimes think this poet
has struck a higher chord of music than any who pre-

ceded him. To him more than to any other of those
who voice their moods in verse, there seems to have
been given the faculty to penetrate the profounder depths
of feeling, to play more subtle melodies upon the soul
of man, to look down deeper into elemental emotions,
to lift a little while the mystic veil, and gaze upon a
beauty vague and terrible, as that which haunts the
dreams of those who sleep in graveyards. To those
who read his verse there comes consciousness of profounder and diviner things than those perceptible to
eyes blinded and dim with dust blown from the highways
of the earth, he wakes the seventh sense and shows us
spectral soulscapes of unearthly beauty. The intellectual atmosphere is redolent with the perfume of invisible
flowers, music of invisible orchestras, visions of the
mystical realm which

> . . . lies in heaven across the flood
>   Of ether as a bridge.
> Beneath the tides of day and night,
>   With flame and darkness ridge.

He seemed to see beyond the horizon of human perception, and piercing dusty mists with eyes of fire, gaze
into the heart of the invisible. It was not enough for
him to see the things that others see, or know the joys
that gladdened other eyes, and thrilled the chords of
souls not less than his with deep pulsations of immortal
passion, and joy of mortal life and ecstasy of wind and
wave and star. It was not enough for him to absorb
into his soul the beauty and the verdure of the earth,
and weave into the fibre of his verse the white and

ashen splendour of the dawn, the golden glory of the
noonday sun, the sacred dusk of twilight. No. He
would absorb them all indeed—and wait—so impatiently
for the night—for the night to come with its darkness—
and in the bosom of the darkness the stars—and from
the hearts of the stars, the music—that music astral and
divine—the music of the star-beams singing, and join
his voice to theirs and sing

> a song whose hair
> Blows like a flame and blossoms like a wreath,

till they who read his verse when the moon is high in
the heavens and the astral light of the singing spheres
floats earthwards so mysteriously, can sometimes hear in
sweetest fancy the tinkle of angelic harps and hear the
seraphim sweetly singing as they cluster in the twilight
of the immortal heavens to sing immortal songs.

It is this transcendental tone—this poetic perception
of the supersensible—which gives this poet a place apart
from his fellows.   He seems to have touched a higher
chord—subtle, attenuated and refined—some prelude of
a sublimer minstrel—a stray note of a choir celestial—
a floating melody which drifted downwards to lift us
upwards along the aisles of light to realms forever divine,

> Where we shall meet
> With bodiless form and unapparent feet.

The soul of man looks out of his prison-house of clay
and waking strangely from the sleep of life holds cosmic
communion with nature unconcealed and feels a deep

and subtle affinity with all that is beautiful and fair—
the sweet roses—its sisters—its brothers, the stars.
From the tragic island of his frail mortality he drifts
in dreams to glory and with an inner ear hears sweeter
harmonies than those poor muffled sounds which mocked
him in the midnight of mortality. On waves of colour,
sound, and light, he floats to sweetest rapture and is
absorbed in the depths of that supreme Being whose
mortal mood he was.

Rossetti buried his happiness some years before he
died and, as students of his biography know, he buried
his poetry with her. There is no more pathetic picture
in all literary biography than that which was visible to
the eyes of those who saw a broken-hearted poet enter
the room where the love of his heart lay dead, and after
reading to ears that were deaf the poems he wrote to
her honour, deposit in the coffin the book of verse
which she had been the ever living inspiration. Later,
the body was exhumed and the only copy of the poems
then extant was rescued from oblivion ; and those who
read these verses sometimes think they have absorbed
the spirit of the dead and still retain with all its ecstasy
of love some odour likewise of the grave, the coffin
and the dust wherein they lay a time upon a pallid
breast. Others who read them think that when the
spirit parted from the clay, she took these lines with
her to heaven to be revised by angels and dowered with
perennial immortality by the warm breath of gods. But
this is only fancy. On her death the poet strove to
voice his grief in those sonnets of the Book of Life—
sonnets which sometimes seem to sweat a sweat of

blood, which glow and palpitate and tremble with the
very ecstasy of music and blush and thrill like things
of flesh and blood.   The lines are dripping with tears
and damp with vermilion drops.

> His soul remembers yet
> The sunless hours that pass it by
> And still he hears the Night's disconsolate cry
> And feels the branches ringing wet
> Cast on his brow that may not once forget
> Dumb tears from the blind sky.

The dew of death was on his brow some years before
he died, and the relentless grip of an insidious disease
drove him for peace to poison.   Through the clouds of
chloral and mists of tears the splendid soul shone like
a star, and even as the microbe ate away the ropes of dust
that bound the spirit and the flesh, his eyes forever open
sought the light that fadeth not forever.   Through the
long hours of the night when pain denied him sleep he
paced with restless step his studio and watched the
first faint streaks of dawn fall on the picture that he
loved.

> Look in my face—my name is Might Have-Been.
> I am also called—No More—Too Late—Farewell
> Up to thine ear I hold the dead sea shell.

There is no biography but autobiography, no revelation but self-revelation.   Where shall we seek the character of an author?   We must seek for it in his writings.
The spirit of the author broods over his creations.   His
presence is visible between the lines.   We hear his

heart beats in its melodies. Through the flame-lit aisles of the Inferno stalks the majestic figure of Dante. Milton walks in the Garden of Eden, and Homer dogs the footsteps of Achilles. Behind the fantastic figures which revel in the midnight saturnalia of Walpurgis we see the sphinx-like countenance of Goethe. The sunset falls on Scottish hills and from a lonely cottage on the heather the face of Burns looks up and smiles forever. The skylark soars and Shelley sings. The raven sits on every bust of Pallas and the voice of Poe forever echoes in the ringing and the rolling and the tolling of the bells. The dark clouds brood above the heights of Sinai and the thunderings and the lightnings of some immortal wrath stir the spirit of Isaiah to prophesy. The blessed Damozel leans out of heaven, her lily-white hands are on the golden bars, and her eyes look softly downwards

Like waters hushed at even ;

and that white soul which gazes ever upwards, straining against the prison bars of clay in the dim ecstasy of breathless expectation and the vague wonder of divinest discontent—that is Rossetti.

The Fall of the Curate.

THE curate rose from his knees and turned out the lights on the altar. This was the work of the sexton, but the sexton had gone home and there was no one left in the church—none but the curate and the organist—the organist who sat in the shadow of his instrument dreamily fingering the keys.

"Come, Morell," said the curate; "we must close up the church and go home."

"Wait," said the organist softly. "Turn out the lights and wait."

The curate looked at him wonderingly as he sat half concealed in the shadows that enveloped the organ and chancel in a dim, religious mist. He was a strange man, this organist, but a superb musician, of whom apart from that he knew very little. He was a strange man and had made a strange request, and one which in that holy place and hour grated harshly on the tired nerves of a curate already weak and overstrained by the prolonged Lenten services of fasting, and vigil, and prayer. The great body of the church was already shrouded in darkness, with the exception of the light which shone from a few jets of gas on the chancel, whose feeble and uncertain rays, striving ineffectually to relieve the gloom, succeeded only in accentuating the dim fantasy of the shadows which played around the organ and mocked the pale and spectral light that fell on aisle, and altar, and nave. The strange and depressing influence of this environment, combined with the weariness begot of prolonged Lenten labor, stirred the gentle spirit of the curate to revolt against this sudden attack upon his nerves.

"I am tired," he said petulantly. "I have fasted for forty days and worked very hard in the parish. To-morrow (Good Friday) I must rise at seven. Let me go home and rest."

"I have a confession to make," said the organist. "Put out the lights and listen."

There was a strange thrill in the voice of the organist, which moved the curate to wonder—moved him to wonder and fear. With a nervous glance at his companion he passed reluctantly to the lights and extinguished them one by one, with the exception of the solitary jet which burned by the side of the musician in the shadow of the organ. His hand trembled as he touched the jets and his nervousness grew with the darkness which thickened and deepened around him, seeming to stifle him with its closeness and blackness, and oppressing him with a consciousness of some hidden and terrible danger. The last light was extinguished, and nervous and faint and exhausted he sank into a seat in the choir and gazed with strained and expectant eyes at the vague and shadowy figure that sat motionless in front of the organ. But no sound disturbed the stillness; the moments seemed longer than hours and the silence as dense as the darkness which oppressed the soul of the listener with a nameless and terrible fear.

A white hand fluttered in the air—fluttered a moment and fell—and suddenly upon the quiet of the holy place

there burst a flood of most unholy sound. It was a
valse. Wave after wave and tide on tide of sacrilegious
music beat the air, pealing and vibrating through the
hollows of the chancel and rushing in fierce derision
down the dark vistas of the aisles. It mounted to the
galleries and rang among the rafters, storming the altar,
and choir, and chancel with wild harmonic laughter and
musical sneer and jeer, deriding the holiness of the
temple and mocking the sanctity of the sanctuary with
fierce melodic scorn.

"Be silent, madman," cried the curate; "remember
where you are, the place, the hour."

"Be silent, you," cried the organist above the waves
of sound. "Be silent you and listen. It is thus I have
lived my life."

The curate shuddered and bowed his head. The
long Lenten fast had told on his emaciated frame. He
was faint, and weak, and exhausted by the hard work of
the parish, long days of watching by the beds of the sick,
and nights of spiritual striving, and vigil, and fast, and
prayer. But the long Lent battle was drawing to an
end and he had hoped to rest—to rest and be happy;
and now at the moment of his greatest weakness, just
when the battle was over and the victory seemed to be
won; when, weakened and worn by the struggle, he had
hoped to find rest and peace—now, at the moment of
his greatest weakness, the tempter was upon him. The
evil one assailed him in the darkness of the church.
Sin with her sweetest voice was singing as the sirens
sang of old—singing of life and its joy.

Profane and beautiful, the music thrilled his soul,

drowning the whispers of his conscience with hot harmonic waves and waking passions and yearnings he had
never known before.   Passionate and persuasive, it
echoed through the aisles and corridors of his brain and
stormed his soul with waves of fire and melody and light,
as it had stormed and scorned the altar of the church
wherein he knelt and prayed.   For it was singing now
of all life's sweetest joys, its passion and its ecstasy and
hope—the lips that lure, the smile that slays, the hope
that dares and ventures all, the faith that dies forever to
live an hour, and the fathomless love that loses all
to win a little and loves that little better than the lost.
In tender tones and low it told of stolen joys and veiled
and secret bliss, and rapture born of the red, red wine,
and purple passions, and pleasures fierce and fair.
Hark to the voice of Juliet singing a love song to her
Romeo—a love song in the moonlight.   A nightingale
is calling to her mate—the song of the loved to her
lover.   Mark the royal rage of Othello—it is pealing,
pealing, pealing from the organ.   No, it is Ophelia now
who weeps and whispers.   Come.   How the music
thrills and trembles, soft and sweet, tender and low,
tender and low, and soft and sweet, waking a wild delirium of emotional passion and longing in the soul of
him who hears.

   " The world is fair," cries the organ.   " The world is
fair, fair, fair.   Why are you wasting the dawn of your
life in helpless longing and hopeless prayer, when all the
world is fair, fair, fair ? "

   The curate heard and trembled for his soul.   The
contagion of passion had seized him, and he longed to

feel what he heard, to go out of the darkness and gloom of the church into the beautiful world—the purple world, the world of passion, and smiles, and tears, and sunligh·, gold and glory.

The white hand fluttered a moment in the air—fluttered a moment and fell—and rested in silence on the keys. The voice of the organ was hushed, but still the music trembled and thrilled, thrilled in the soul of the curate. A thousand passions hitherto undreamt of vibrated in his heart and strange desires blossomed in his breast. His eye had glanced along the glowing chords of melody and seen the vistas of a larger life.

The organist rose from the organ. His face was pale and sad and his eyes were full of fear as he glanced at the fire in the eyes of the white wan face before him.

"You are going," said the curate.

"Yes, I am going to Sullivan's to gamble and dance and drink," said the musician.

"May I come?" said the curate.

The organist turned away his head and answered hoarsely, "Come."

And they passed from the church together.

The Terrible Tale.

IT lay on the table before him and he almost trembled to touch it—the terrible thing he had written. In the delicate shade of the twilight it seemed to glow and quiver—to tremble and glow and quiver—as though a living spirit moved within.

What had he done? Could it possibly be that he—he—had written this thing? this terrible tale of elemental passion; this unholy revelation of life's divinest secret; this weird brain blossom from esoteric gardens; a spirit spark from never-dying fires; forbidden fruit of intellectual Edens—so bitter-sweet, so terrible, so tender; a tragic-comic flash of joy and sorrow; a glimpse into the mysteries of mysteries; a vision of the holiest of holies; this lightning flash of elemental passion, surcharged with love, and joy, and hate, and music, shedding unholy light on secret places and stirring slumbering hopes and fears to life and action. He had felt like a beautiful god when he wrote it, and flaming melodies ran through his veins and flashed in wild electric music down his arms, and blossomed from his pen in words that laughed, and sobbed, and sighed, and smiled, and blushed, and thrilled in golden toned and purple-hued emotion. He formed them in sentences like battalions and bade them go forth and win him a crown and a sceptre. Ah, how eager he was that that terrible tale should be told—but now—

Now he was haunted by a fear that someone might

read it. Strange eyes might gaze upon it, and weaker
souls than his be seared and branded for eternity by a
sudden consciousness of truth they could not bear.   It
was a moral story, but the morality was in advance of
the times, and he was vaguely conscious that the average
intellect had not evolved sufficiently to appreciate the
deeper truths it taught.

Why had he written this thing?   What had the public
done to him that he should shatter their cherished de-
lusions and bid their gods unveil?   Why should he
open invisible doors and tell unacceptable things? Why
should he snap their cherished chains and bid a crawling generation stand erect when chains were considered
becoming and crawling was essential to happiness?
They who delighted in darkness would resent the intrusion
of light.   The truth so beautiful to him was a terrible
tale to them.

"Their eyes will grow green when they read it," he said
"They will feel wicked.   They will lose their appetites.
They will be driven to desperation and patent medi-
cines."

A ripple of silvery laughter seemed to thrill the manuscript before him, and the spirits he had made seemed
to be wickedly rejoicing together at the mischief they
would work among mankind.

"I must burn it," he said with a shudder.   "Good
heavens! what would happen if anyone were to read
it?"

He walked to the fire—then paused.

"Shall I rob posterity?" he said.

The step of a policeman echoed on the pavement outside. He shuddered with sudden recollection of the fact that this was only the nineteenth century. The delicate irony of the situation brought a pathetic laugh to his lips and he looked at the story which lay in his hand, half-lovingly, half in fear.

" It is so beautiful," he said, " that none will believe it ; so true that all will denounce it, and self-defence compels me to destroy it ; and yet—"

The lines of the manuscript seemed to glow like flames before his eyes, exhaling a subtle odor of passion, and joy, and love—and devilishness.

" I give the fire to the fire," he said, and cast it in the flames.

A Poet-Politician.

IN an age when patriotism is practised as a pro-
fession and sentiment is studied as a science, it is
refreshing to review the career of a man who could
be loyal without the assistance of firecrackers and brave
in the absence of a band.

At the name of Mazzini visions of daggers float before the Tory eye. Was he not the arch-conspirator of
the nineteenth century? Was he not the terrible revolutionist who, exiled from his own country for rebellion
against foreign despotism and monarchical tyranny, established in every city of Europe secret societies of
assassins to hide in dark holes and shadowy corners and
stab the unsuspecting aristocrat unawares? Was he not
the brain of a vast conspiracy which aimed at the over-
throw of the divine institution of monarchy and the
sacred oligarchy of priestcraft, which planted dynamite
bombs under every throne in Europe and had its spies
and agents in every land and every rank of society. If
a king grew sick of overeating (as even the most divinely appointed king will do) suspicion cried, Mazzini and
poison. If the masses of any country so far forgot their
position as to demand liberty of speech, suspicion cried
Mazzini and anarchy. If some wretched toiler, crushed
like a worm beneath the heel of privilege, ventured like
a worm to turn, society, horrified at his impudence, cried,
Mazzini and revolution. He was held responsible for
every outrage ; he was the root of riot, he was the source

of sin, he was the sower of sedition, he was the parent of republicanism, the voice of revolution, the Nemesis of monarchy. How many worthy aristocrats have peered under their beds before retiring to rest to see if a representative of Mazzini was there? How many stately dames have gathered within the walls of their venerable castle and told in horror-stricken tones of the heretical purposes and fearful methods of the countrymen of Borgia, De Medici and Machiavelli?

If the same providence which made Italy is also responsible for the existence of the Italians, it must be given credit for the possession of an infinite irony not altogether consistent with popular conceptions of the divine character. I presume, however, that within the compass of the nature of providence, there is room, if not for sin at least for satire, and that it was under the influence of this mood, or else a unique benevolence too subtle for poor humanity to appreciate, that the powers, whose function it is to fashion worlds, were constrained to ordain perpetual anarchy in an earthly paradise.

The history of Italy has been a succession of tragedies ; there is hardly a spot of her soil that has not been saturated with blood. The loveliness of the land was its ruin. Its very beauty attracted barbarians from afar to feed on its fruits and luxuriate in the soft splendor of its valleys. One by one the conquerors of Europe have trampled on the land which once had Europe at its feet. Hardly had the tide of the invasion of Attila and his Huns rolled back from the ruins of the Alps by the eunuch Narses, when the Lombards, under their king Alboni, swept into the unfortunate country, to be

in turn conquered and supplanted by Charlemagne and
his Franks. Even the Saracens invaded the country
and wrested tribute from the pope. Lovely valleys and
fertile fields were devastated and reduced to sterility by
the fierce incursions of the Northmen and Magyars.
The Carlovingian kings were succeeded by a line of
Italians, whose rule was practically only nominal and
gave abundant opportunity for the growth of feudal and
civic power. The great nobles in the provinces and the
great merchants and bishops in the cities founded parties
and factions, and inaugurated that bitter series of civil
contentions which for many centuries filled the country
with internal strife.

In 962 the crown of Italy was seized by Otto, the
German, and two centuries later that foolish burlesque
on ancient grandeur, the Holy Roman Empire, was
born. The twelfth century witnessed the beginning of
the bitter struggle between the Guelphs and Ghibellines
and the advent of Frederick Barbarossa, to reduce the
growing power of the Italian cities. During this and
the succeeding century the country was the scene of
perpetual strife. When the people were not warring
with some foreign power, they were engaged in bitter
civil contentions, and suffering from self-inflicted wounds.
The rivalries of factions, of princes, of nobles, of cities,
and of provinces generated unceasing wars. Remnants
of the many races that had overrun the country still lingered
in localities to breed contention. By the fifteenth century,
Italy was divided among five leading powers—the Papacy,
Naples, Milan, Florence, and Venice. The last two
republics for some time managed, on account chiefly of

their commercial advantages, to preserve an isolated greatness, but this was as evanescent as it was glorious, and in the succeeding centuries their power declined. The condition of Italy in the fifteenth century was aggravated by the invasion of the French, and the country became a short time later a battle-ground for the rival forces of Francis I. and Charles V. In the sixteenth century it became largely subject to Spain, and for the next hundred years was alternately in the possession of several European powers. At the close of the eighteenth century, this unfortunate country, which had lain at the feet of nearly every conqueror in Europe, felt upon its bleeding soil the mighty tread of the greatest of all conquerors and saw the meteoric genius of Napoleon flash like a glittering star across the horizon of its history.

In 1805, Napoleon was crowned King of Italy. After the Congress of Vienna, the country was restored to its original position and practically became subject to Austria. The princes, who exercised absolute powers and mercilessly punished all attempts at reform, independence or self-government on the part of the people. A powerful Austrian army was stationed in Lombardo-Venetia, to aid any of the princes who might need its assistance to crush and control the people ; the Italians had absolutely no part in the control of their own country and were severely punished if they ventured to de. mand it, or even to complain of the misery generated by political despotism. The discontent of the masses found vent in secret societies, of which the greatest was the Carbonari. Several risings took place against Austrian despotism, but were suppressed with great cruelty and the leaders punished by death.

Such was the condition of Italy at the time of the birth and boyhood of Mazzini. We see him first as an enthusiastic student at Genoa, poring over the classics, reading the pages of Tacitus, wandering by the shores of the beautiful sea with Plutarch in his hand, and drinking in with pride and wonder the marvellous story of the rise and glory and achievements of the great Romans of old. One does not need to be an Italian to sympathize with the passionate indignation of the young student when he compared the ancient glory of his country with its modern degradation. Even a stranger, who, unlike himself, could claim no relationship with the immortals, can readily appreciate the deep emotion of the countryman of the Cæsars when he read of the mighty deeds of his ancestors and stood in startled wonder before the pictured glory of those days when old Rome sat enthroned upon her seven hills, crowned queen of the ancient world, and sent forth her Cæsars to conquer and her Ciceros to charm. What vision of vanished glory must have passed before the mind of the dreamer as he sat, Plutarch in hand, on some high cliff by the shores of the happy sea. Visions of the imperial eagles sweeping through distant forests, riding on stormy seas, flashing triumphant in battle, and passing through danger and darkness, conquering and to conquer through the world. Visions of Scipio on the ruins of Carthage, of Titus on the ruins of Jerusalem, of Pompey sweeping the Mediterranean, of Cæsar crossing the Rubicon. Visions of the magnificent city in the days of its antique splendor, its mighty streets lined with marble statues of those that had made it glorious, its stately palaces standing in pillared beauty by the way, its mighty Forum where the destinies of innumerable nations were determined. Visions of Cicero pleading with divine eloquence in the Forum. Visions of the mighty Coliseum with its gladiatorial combats and its benches thronged with the figures of the conquerors of the world. Visions of the mighty empire, which, extending on all sides of the imperial city, held in supreme subjection Gaul and German, Hun and Vandal, Jew and Egyptian, Grecian and Briton and innumerable other peoples in Europe and Africa and Asia. Visions of those all-conquering cohorts against which the bravest armies of mighty peoples dashed themselves in vain, for the destruction of which the prayers of the Druid to the gnarled god of the forest, of the Jew to the veiled presence of Jehovah, of the Greek to the supreme power of Jove, of the Egyptian to the might of Osiris, were all offered up in vain. Visions of the imperial mistress of war supreme over all men and all their gods, and holding them all at her feet.

Such were the pictures that rose before the eye of the student Mazzini when his mind dwelt on the past, but sadly different was the scene he saw when, rising from his dreams, he looked around him. He saw his country subject to a foreign power, his countrymen denied freedom of speech, freedom of thought and freedom of action. He saw them bowed down, humiliated and scorned. He saw the armed soldiers of Austria in his city and hardly dared even to whisper the love that filled his heart for Italy, the hatred he felt for her foes. He

heard of frequent rebellions of his hot-tempered countrymen against the government, and sometimes saw their
dead bodies dragged through the streets or hanging on
the scaffold. As the Italians were denied all freedom of
speech in public, they naturally were forced to form
secret societies for the purpose of meeting together and
devising means for the liberation of their country. The
bluff, open-minded Briton may sneer at the "under-
hand" methods of these patriots, but he should not
forget the fact that this method of warfare was forced
upon the people by the despotism which forbade and
punished every other form of assembly. There was no
other alternative open. The patriots must meet in secret
or not meet at all.

In the year 1829 Mazzini allied himself with the Carbonari feeling, however distrustful of their methods he
might be, that in the ranks of that society alone would
he find the opportunity which he desired to assist in the
liberation of his country. But the government were too
familiar with the methods and too fearful of the purposes
of this famous organization to neglect submitting it to a
severe and perpetual scrutiny, and Mazzini soon found
to his cost that not even the rigid formula of the secret
ritual, or the severe rites of initiation, were adequate to
protect the society from the intrusion of spies. It is not
unlikely that secret agents of the government were
present in every lodge of the conspirators, and the most
guarded and reticent patriot was in perpetual danger of
betrayal. A short time after he had joined the Carbonari, Mazzini was betrayed to the police and cast into

prison at Savona. His employment here strikingly
illustrated the quaint words of the poet :

"Stone walls do not a prison make
Nor iron bars a cage."

His body was imprisoned but not his mind. It was
while confined to this cell that he formulated his future
methods of political procedure. It was there that he
saw, as in a vision, the picture of a great united Italy,
free from coercion, free from division, and free from the
curse of oppression ; there he dreamt that beautiful
dream, which came also to Dante in his night, which
has for many weary centuries been the inspiration and
the joy of the poets and patriots of the stricken land—
the dream of a nation awakening from its sleep, casting
its fetters from its limbs and rising again to those sublime
proportions, which made it once the pride and glory of
the world. On his release from prison Mazzini organized the "Young Italy Association." The purpose
of this society was to achieve the liberty and union
of the provinces of Italy and establish that country as an
independent nation under a republican form of government. The aspirations of the patriots were not confined
to the redemption of their own country. They wished
to establish in Italy a model nation, an example to the
other nations of Europe, a type on which the democrats
of Europe would see the ideal to which they might bring
their own nations to conform. Mazzini was essentially
an idealist. He aspired to liberate the continent from
the despotism of feudal institutions, and establish a new
and happier era of popular government, fraternity, union

and peace.   To the realization of this ideal his life was
henceforth consecrated, and till the day of his death he
toiled and fought, wrote, exhorted, plotted and suffered,
that his dream might be written in indelible characters
on the face of the land that he loved.   The reward of
his early exertions was a sentence of perpetual banish-
ment, and from the year 1832 he was an outlaw from Italy.
Henceforth for many years his life was spent in hiding.
To all but his most intimate associates his whereabouts
was generally unknown.   Despite the secrecy of his life,
his energy never ceased.   In some mysterious way he
seemed to communicate with all parts of his own country
and of Europe and to organize and direct that remarkable succession of conspiracies and agitations and of
revolutionary ideas which made him the terror · of all
governments and the idol of all republicans.

          .   .   .   .

The discontent in Italy burst into revolution in Lom-
bardy in 1848, and Mazzini returned to that country to
assist Garibaldi in leading and directing the forces of
the revolutionists.   Attempts on the part of the King of
Sardinia to bribe him by the offer of the position of
Prime Minister of a new state of Piedmont-Lombardy,
he rejected with scorn.   He struggled bravely against
the powerful forces of government, and even after the
surrender of Milan, still toiled and schemed to maintain
the contest in the Alps.   Failing in this, he went to
Tuscany.   His vast popularity with his countrymen was
amply evidenced by the passionate and enthusiastic welcome he received at Leghorn and other places where
he was recognized.   He was elected a deputy to the

Republican Congress at Rome, and he and Armellina and Saffi were appointed a triumvirate with powers to govern the city as they pleased. From a political point of view, Mazzini was at this time probably at the summit of his greatness He was the idol of the Romans, and practically the absolute head of an Italian Republic. But his position, however exalted it might appear, was in reality far from enviable ; the forces at his disposal were weak and undisciplined, the fortifications of the city were of small strength. His camp was filled with spies and many of his supporters lacked only the opportunity to become traitors. A strong French army was marching against the city to replace the Pope on his throne. What a Napoleon, an Alexander or a Cæsar would have done under circumstances like these, it is difficult to say. It is possible, perhaps, they might by some supreme expedient of genius, have overcome the manifold difficulties about them, defeated the French, marched swiftly on their other foes and routed them, established the new Republic on a firm basis, organized a powerful army, reconquered all Italy, defeated or conciliated Austria and France and re-established by force of genius the Republic of Italy. To accomplish such a tremendous task as this required, however, a genius and military capacity of so supreme a quality as is rarely given to man. Mazzini, brave, noble, eloquent, as he proved himself to be, was not a Cæsar. After a short and stubborn resistance, the French entered Rome and re-placed the Pope on his beloved throne. The triumvirs resigned and left the city and Mazzini returned to London. Again he had failed to liberate Italy but he did

not despair of her freedom.   He organized the Society
of the Friends of Italy and also the European Society,
and busied himself contriving new plots and seeking
new schemes to destroy foreign influence and monarchy
in Italy.   He planned and organized risings in Mantua,
Genoa, Leghorn and Milan.   When the heroic Garibaldi
undertook his famous expedition against Sicily and Naples,
Mazzini spared no exertion to furnish it with all available
essentials of success.   When the army of the patriots
were dispersed at Aspromonte, the profound indignation
of Mazzini at the conduct of the King prompted him to a
violent and eloquent attack on the Sardinian monarchy.
The reply to this was a sentence of death.   The con-
vention of September, 1860, the crowning triumph of
the genius of Cavour was denounced by Mazzini as an
unworthy compromise.   In 1869 he was banished for a
second time from Switzerland, where he had taken
refuge, and the next year he was arrested and cast
into prison at Gaeta.   On his liberation he lived for a
time at Lugano, and on March, 1872, his weary, tortured life came to a close, and he breathed his last at
Pisa and was buried in the land he loved far better than
life.

Such is the story of Mazzini, and a sadder, sweeter,
grander life than his was never lived by man.   I have
given the bare outline of events, but who can tell the
secret history of his thoughts and life, who can picture
in cold type the terrible strength of that passion which
could survive a thousand failures and see hope in the
darkest night.   Who can measure the might of that
devotion at whose bidding he gladly, lovingly, laid down

his peace, his prosperity, his rest, his life, upon the consecrated altar of an almost hopeless cause. The secret
history of the life of Mazzini has never been written.
We read of the events, the revolution, the conspiracies,
the visible evidences of his activity, but we know nothing
of the terrible toil, the planning and scheming and
contriving which brought these things to pass ; nothing
of the strange meetings in dark cellars ; the gatherings
in hidden places, the meetings in strange caves by
lonely Italian shores ; the assembling in mountain
gorges of those ostracized conspirators, to whom the
slightest revelation of their activity meant death. We
know nothing of the spinning, the weaving, and winding of the mysterious web of giant conspiracies of the
secret language of signs and symbols by which the
rebels communicated in public ; the fierce, swift councils held in lonely corners by the light of some dimly
burning fire. Of these we know nothing, nor do we
know anything of that internal, mental strife, that nameless sorrow with which the hunted patriot, driven from
land to land, banished from the presence of light by
the blood-hounds of the monarchs of Europe, looked
down on the wrecks of shattered hopes, and mourned
in secret tribulation the death of cherished dreams.
To build, to weave, to scheme, to elaborate a plot, to
see it budding into form beneath his subtle hands and
then to learn that it had falled through treachery of
friends or force of foes, this was the repeated experience
of Mazzini. Who shall tell of the strength of that love
which could outlive the death of many hopes ; who can
record the tempests of his thoughts or tell of the doubts

he defeated, the sins he smote, the cares he conquered ?

Mazzini was not the only weaver of plots for the liberation of Italy. In another and higher sphere a giant mind laid other and deeper plans whose fruit was the freedom and union of Italy. I shall not attempt in this short sketch to describe the character or follow in its intricate and winding ways the profound policy of one who was probably the greatest statesman of modern Italy. To Cavour must be given the supreme credit for the union and freedom of Italy. He was more patient, more cautious, calmer, less scrupulous, than Mazzini or Garibaldi. He was willing to take liberty in fractions, to fight for a little at a time, to temporize, to compromise, to acquiesce, to adapt himself to circumstances, until by so doing he was enabled to attain a power by which he could control circumstances and adapt them in time to his will. Instead of alienating the government by expressing his opinions, he conciliated it by concealing them. Having thus won the confidence of the ruling powers, he mounted upon it to office. He never attempted the impossible. He wasted no strength where it would be ineffectual. While Mazzini, banished for his imprudence, sought to undermine the foundations of the fortress, and Garibaldi battered at is walls, Cavour remained inside and mixed with its defenders, learnt their secrets, studied their methods, won their confidence, became their leader, and, having thus obtained control of the fortress, handed it over to freedom. What his real opinions were no man knows, for he loved them too well to express them. He was probably as great a patriot as Mazzini, but he knew the times and seasons too well to sow seeds on frozen ground. His profound plots, his deep intrigues, his consummate diplomacy, created those complications which forced Austria to withdraw from Italy. By masking his patriotism he preserved it for future use. He had his agents in every state in Italy and every court in Europe. He scorned no means of attaining his ends, played on the animosities of individuals and the rivalries of nations, and used all manner of instruments, from Garibaldi to the ladies of the court. He critically estimated to what degree of weakness his opponents must be reduced before a blow would be effectual. While the hot-headed 'patriots made fruitless attacks on the army of Austria and tried by force of arms to drive it from the country, Cavour looked deeper than they. He knew that the army was only an instrument obedient to orders. Who gave the orders? Certain men in Vienna. Who were these men, what were there motives, what their character, to what influences were they susceptible, what was the weakness of each? This was his business to find, and having found, to use for Italy. He knew that the forces of the Italians were not sufficiently powerful in themselves to drive the Austrians from Italy, but he also knew that, however weak his countrymen might be alone, they became formidable as auxiliaries of other powers. He must form an alliance with France or some other nation. Seeing that the energies of the revolutionists were divided, he determined to unite them. What were the influences antagonistic to union? Each king and each state was subject to some controlling influences. In one it was ambition, in another avarice, in another a woman, in another a priest. He must have spies in each court, agents in every palace ; statesmen, sweethearts, and valets, all must serve his ends and receive their instructions from him, and so he wove his webs. At the same time he weakened the temporal power of the Pope. He outwitted the rulers of a Church which was represented at every court and in many royal households of Europe. He mastered with their own weapons, and in the very centre of their power, the keenest masters of intrigue in Europe. He undermined the papal power, conquered the Jesuits with their own subtle weapons, foiled Antonelli, and with the most perfect courtesy ruined Romanism in Italy, where it is now only a name.

But while to Cavour is conceded the immediate credit for the union and liberation of Italy, to Mazzini there must also be conceded the honour of having awakened in the hearts of his countrymen that passionate patriotism and fearless courage in the expression of their convictions, which, if it did not in itself cause the destruction of Austrian power in Italy, was at least instrumental in proving to the Austrians that they could only retain the country at a vast expenditure of blood and money. Had the repeated revolts which Mazzini instigated and organized not convinced Austria of the difficulty of ruling the country, it is possible that, despite the efforts of Cavour, she might have attempted the task for half a century longer. Towards the union of Italy Mazzini also contributed in no small degree. He united the people in a common cause, before Cavour united them in a common country. He found that sentiment of loyalty to Italy, without which its union could never have been consummated, and which, far more than any constitutions or statutes found an enduring basis of union. He made them Italians in heart before they became Italians in fact. He organized branches of his society in every state, he taught the same holy lesson to all and in the heart of each he planted a blossom from the everlasting flower of his faith.

He was a poet-politician and around him there has been long the halo of romance. He early dreamt a beautiful dream and waking to a tortured day kept ever before his love-lit eyes the perfect picture of his pure ideal. He often failed but never faltered. In darkest night or dreariest day, when the fires of hope burnt low and the picture of his idolized country stretched bleeding on her cross, rose darkly before his weary eyes, he still stretched out his hands to save her, revived her with his tears, fed her with his blood. His life was the life of a martyr. Not only did he suffer sorrow, poverty, pain and loss in person, but every blow that fell on Italy pierced him to his heart. He was one with his country and whenever she suffered he sighed, feeling her pains repeated in himself. His fidelity was perfect, no power could weaken his faith, though all were tried. The glitter of gold, the promise of peace, the power of princes, the danger of death, the wiles of priests, the edicts of governments, failure, poverty, exile, all failed to shake his allegiance to republicanism, his deathless love of Italy.

He was worthy of the Romans of old, worthy of Reg-

ulus, worthy of Cato, worthy of Gracchus, worthy of
Brutus. When in the capital of the new Italy another
pantheon arises and the statues of noble Romans are re-
placed upon the pedestals from which the impious hand
of the conqueror had cast them down, they will not
stand alone. By the side of Regulus, and in the companionship of Gracchus, fit associate alike of Cato and
of Cicero, there will stand the pictured bust of the
patriot Mazzini, and if any ask the reason of his presence
there it will be told to them that he was the man whose
ever flowing tears and bleeding heart so fertilized the
soil of Italy that it brought forth men like the men that
it bore of old, who, standing by his side, freed their
country and prepared for Italy a future worthy of her
skies.

He has redeemed this century from the charge of
mediocrity of sentiment. His beautiful, bla.neless life
consecrated to the service of a dream, will prove to the
posterity that the present generation was not wholly des-
titute of heroism. He has robbed antiquity of its monopoly of the heroic. A beautiful dreamer, he proved to
the world that the things which are dreamt can be, that
into the darkness of dust the glory of spirit can flow.
Over the bowed figure of a toil-worn generation, over the
wrecks of shattered faiths, the palsied forms of senile sentiments, the smouldering fires of smitten hopes, his spirit
passed like a fresh breath of life, and they awoke. Like
the opening anthem of a great drama, like the music of an
unfolding world, like the perfect voice of an angel incarnate proclaiming a new heaven and a new earth, we

hear again his passionate words to the republicans of Europe :

" From our cross of sorrow and persecution, we men of exile, representatives in heart and faith of the enslaved millions of men, proclaim the religion of a new epoch.   Let not the hateful cry of reaction be heard upon your lips but hearken to the sweet and solemn words of the days that are to be.   Have faith, O ye who suffer for a noble cause, apostles of a truth the world comprehends not, warriors in a sacred fight whom ignorance calls rebels.   To-morrow, perhaps, the world, now incredulous, will bow before you in holy enthusiasm. —the sublime cry of Galileo, ' Eppar si muove ' will float above the ages.   Child of Humanity, raise thy brow to the sun of God and read upon the heavens, Faith and action.   The future is ours."

Utophia.

Utophia, beautiful city of dreams,
  When will the eyes of men behold thee
Arise like a wonderful star in the night
    From the mists that enshroud and enfold
    thee?
Thy mansions aglow with the light of the morning,
  Thy temples aflame with the beauty to be,
The light of thy presence forever adorning
  A race everlastingly free.

Long, long have we waited in darkness and sorrow
  With eyes that are aching and heavy with
    tears,
Hoping to see thee to-morrow, to-morrow
  Enthroned on the summit of years.
And oft in the night of our vain endeavor
  We have dreamed a dream of a sweeter morn,
Only to waken to toil forever
  In cities forever forlorn.

Cities we have, but we name them never,
  Shadows of shame—forever accurst—
Where the souls of the millions toil forever
  In ceaseless hunger and quenchless thirst.
Down, down in the darkness that never rises
  Crippled and dwarfed in their hopeless graves,
They curse the pitiless fate that disguises
  The souls of men in the bodies of slaves.

And day by day we have toiled and striven,
    Fettered by fate and by folly bound,
Till we saw a light in the darkness given
    Of a city sought for and never found.
Far through the mists of the midnight gleaming
    A beautiful vision met our sight,
Forever to fly when the eyes of our dreaming
    Were opened again to the night.

O city of dreams that are fairer than dreams,
    And hopes that flower—and fade again,
Marvellous mirage that is—or seems
    Forever sought for—in vain
Mock us no longer—but rise in glory
    And crown the conquest that love began
Till the beautiful dream of a beautiful story
    Is the visible dwelling of man.

Utophia, wonderful city of dreams
    I see thy lights ! I see thy lights !
Far where the sun of the morning gleams
    Through the darkest and saddest of nights.
The lights on thy altars are glowing and flaming,
    Thy mansions are thronged with the hosts of
        the free,
And the voice of thy millions is grandly proclaim-
        ing   .
    " The things that are dreamt can be."

The Intruder.

THE statue of the god stood in the garden on his pedestal, erect in marble pride, indifferent to the world, its joys and cares, and splendidly oblivious of the human. The pale rays of the moon fell softly on it, revealing its frozen beauty to the night and showing in quaint relief the smile of fine disdain with which it viewed the mortal underneath, who, with admiring eyes, gazed upwards upon the frozen god.

" Well, Apollo, things have changed since those old Attic days when men and maidens knelt before you and wreathed your brows with flowers."

Was it a fancy—or did the eyelid fall? The stranger, watching the statue, thought he saw a sudden flush of purple on the cheek.

" Men would not worship you to-day if you were still abroad. The world is very civilized and very sordid, very wise and very miserable. Ah, Apollo, can you not come back again ?"

He thought he saw a thin vermilion line, and then another, stand out on the veins of the marble ; then laughed at the folly of his imagination and passed on musingly out of the garden. Step by-step he slowly passed away, but when the last faint step had shed its feeble echo on the air the statue suddenly leaped to life. The marble veins were flushed with blood. The lips grew ruby red. The eyes flashed light, and Apollo, god of the morning, radiant and beautiful, but in a mortal guise, stepped down from his pedestal.

"Mankind are miserable," he said, "and I have slept too long. I will go down and sing sweet songs and make men happy."

Apollo stood upon a hill and looked down upon the city and thrilled with joy to see the golden lights that twinkled in the shadows of the buildings down below with vague suggestion of forbidden mystery. What were they doing there, the restless sons of men whose fathers wreathed his brow with flowers long centuries ago? Whose were the songs they sang? What music moved them? Did beauty thrill them still, and at what altar did they kneel to-day? His heart warmed to the world again as he saw it stretched in visible beauty before him. He would go down and dwell with men once more. Were they unhappy? He would make them happy and sing sweet songs to fill their hearts with joy. Were they exultant? He would share their pleasure and join his happy voice to swell the chorus.

With eager steps he strode towards the city, and soon he stood amid its crowded streets thronged with the hurrying feet of many people who hastened to and fro, intent on business. The world had altered strangely since he left it, and he was much surprired to see the bustle and excitement of the people, and the strained look of care upon their faces as they hurried eagerly he knew not where. What were they seeking? Was it music, sweet sounds, or pictures, flowers, pleasure, beauty, or did they hasten to the shrine of some strange god whose name he did not know? These faces, wrinkled and distorted with weight of some ignoble, sordid passion, filled him with horror as he moved

among them, so strangely different were they from the
faces, bright with the rapture of divine emotion, which
smiled upon him in the old—the ever young—the golden
days gone by when he was god, and man was god-like
and beauty was his bride.

The twilight deepened, and still he moved among
them, filled with pity and bewilderment and terror to
find himself unknown, unloved, unnoticed. And now
and then he paused and touched his harp and lifted up
his voice to sing them songs of an earlier love, a holier
passion ; songs of the seasons—the splendid spring, the
smiling summer, the golden autumn, ripe with decaying
beauty ; songs of the heart, the minstrelsy of love, sweet
lips, soft cheeks, and eyes athrill with passion ; songs of
the soul, the spirit ditties, the heaven-soaring melodies,
the songs celestial, rich with the music of divinest passion—immortal hope, immortal joy, and love immortal.

"So lived they," he murmured, "in the golden days
gone by. So loved they, so sang they, so lived they
steeped in music, in the olden, the golden, the happy
days gone by—in the morning, the sunrise, the dawn-
day of the world—when I was god, and life was melody,
and man was god-like and beauty was his bride."

And as he sang, the strangers gathered around him
and mocked the sunlight dancing in his eyes, and bade
him cease, saying, "Your song disturbs us. We cannot
think, we cannot calculate, nor count, nor cheat, nor
steal, nor live our lives, and do the thousand crafty,
unholy things that gain us cash. Your song is golden
but we cannot coin it."

"This cash must be their god," he muttered, and

ceased to sing, knowing his reign was over. Another god reigned in the human heart, and beauty was an alien in the world. He was a stranger, seeking for joy and offering joy for joy, but wherever he went they asked for cash and called him "vagrant," "idler," and drove him, tired, away, hungry, footsore, from the homes he sought to fill with music. At last he was arrested and brought before the court.

"You are a loafer," said the magistrate. "Have you no business?"

"My business is to make men happy."

"I never heard of that occupation," answered the court. "Can't you do anything practical? Can you make boots, or break stones, or saw wood, or cut out coats, or dig drains, or do anything mechanical? If not, you are a vagrant."

"I can do none of these things," said Apollo, "for I am not a machine nor a brute. I am only a god, and I can only fill the world with music, and sing sweet songs, and tell great tales of gods, and build a temple of delight for men to dwell in, and play rare melodies upon the human heart, and paint upon the brain fair pictures."

"But you cannot dig," cried the magistrate severely. "You cannot dig, nor plough, nor make boots. You are not practical. You are not useful. I send you to prison for life."

And now Apollo lies in prison — the strings of his harp are broken, and who shall hear him sing?

The Yellow Mask.

HE crept up close to the garden wall, and, bending down his head beside a crack, with hungry ears and flashing eyes he listened to the sounds of revelry within. How gay the music sounded as it floated out of the windows and through the trees, mingled with the sound of merry words and silvery laughter from the happy guests within. To a strolling actor out of employment, with an empty pocket and a passionate craving for pleasure, such a scene, at all times enticing, to night was doubly attractive.

"Some of us are princes and some are paupers," he muttered jealously. "How fate mixes us up to be sure, placing the wrong men in the best places. Now, who is there inside who could adorn a ball like I ? "

The sensuous music of a valse, borne to his ears on the warm breeze that floated through the garden, murmured a perfumed invitation in his ear, and stirred his heart with a passionate longing to leave a cheerless world behind and mingle with the guests within. And why should he not ? There was only a wall between them. A sudden impulse moved his heart to join that splendid beauty show of flashing eyes and ringing laughter, and placing his hand upon the wall he climbed and suddenly vaulted over, and cowered in the shadows of the foliage in the park.

"Nothing venture, nothing win," he muttered, as he cowered behind the bushes watching the scene before him. "It is a masquerade—ah, if I only had a mask ! "

The beautiful gardens before him were brilliantly lighted with many colored lanterns, and to and fro along the broad pathways that wound among the flowers and the trees, long lines and groups of guests passed ceaselessly, gaily conversing and brilliantly attired in a great variety of many-colored costumes.

"Fine feathers make fine birds," muttered the actor grudgingly, "but if I only had a few feathers I could soar above them all and be a Romeo to some Juliet and court fortune in an hour."

A step upon the path beside him warned him to be cautious, and hastily drawing back behind the bushes he waited for the stranger to pass by. The path which ran beside his place of vantage was a narrow and winding one leading from the centre of the gardens, and in the imperfect light of a lantern which hung on the trees a short distance away he could see a man and woman coming down it closely masked and very handsomely attired. She was chatting vivaciously and he apparently was walking in moody silence by her side. Suddenly the woman paused and turned to the man beside her with an impatient toss of the head.

"If you would only venture," she said.

"I dare not," he muttered weakly.

"Well, don't, but you know the penalty," she cried in a sudden temper, and turning hastily she walked back the way she had come, while he, instead of following her, stood for a moment irresolutely on the pathway, then sat down on a bench by the bushes and covered his face with his hands.

"Well, that was a pretty miss," muttered the actor to himself as he cowered discontentedly behind the bushes· "Why, the man can't play the lover at all. Ah, if he had only a little of my art he could have done the part to perfection. What a poor-spirited creature it is. I have a fancy to teach him a lesson."

And leaping the bushes suddenly he stood in the centre of the pathway and presented himself with a low bow to the stranger. "Pardon me, sir," he said, "but you did that very badly."

"Did what?" cried the other suddenly, jumping to his feet with a startled look in his eyes and laying his hand on his sword.

"Why, the lover act," said the actor imperturbably. But don't draw, if you please. I am, as you see, unarmed. When she said, 'Will you venture?' you should have bowed thus—gracefully—and said, 'Ay, madame, anything—anything, madame, for you.'"

"Oh, indeed," said the other icily. "Sir, I think you are very presuming."

"And so was Romeo," said the actor enthusiastically, "and you, if you had only presumed a moment ago— but I could have done better myself——"

"You certainly have the nerve," said the other haughtily, then his eye suddenly lighted up as a new thought came to his mind and he murmured softly to himself, "Surely Providence has sent this fellow to save the situation. We look very much alike." Turning to the actor instantly he cried, "I think you have ventured too far already, sir."

A clash of steel broke the silence as his sword, apparently by accident, dropped from his hand on the pavement. In a moment the actor had seized it and pointed it at his throat.

"As far as your throat, my lord," he answered the other quickly, "and if you venture another word I will venture a little farther. Now give me your hat and cloak. I have a fancy to try the lover act myself."

The face of the courtier turned suddenly pale, and then a look of relief passed over it, but he quietly submitted to be bound and gagged, and as the actor assumed the costume and mask of the other he almost fancied he saw a smile on the crafty face before him.

"Our height is about the same," muttered the actor as he threw the cloak over his shoulders. "Our hair is of the same color, and the mask conceals the face, and as to the voice, trust an actor to imitate that. In other particulars we differ, but there I think I have the advantage of your lordship."

A faint smile stole over the pale face of the vanquished courtier as his conqueror bowed gracefully before him, and with a gallant "*Au revoir*, monsieur," strode gaily down the pathway in the direction of the main promenade, in search of the departed Juliet.

.   .   .   .

"The Duke seems very gay to-night," murmured Lady Williams to a lady in a pink mask beside her, as they stood in the centre of the promenade watching a

gallant figure in a yellow mask passing gaily to and fro
among the guests.

"Very gay indeed," the other muttered wonderingly,
"and yet, when I left him a moment ago he certainly
was not gay."

"See! he is coming this way," murmured the other
quickly, and moving slightly to one side she left the
yellow mask and the pink standing together.

"You seem to have recovered your spirits, sir," said
the woman abruptly.

"Now that I see you I am revived," said the other,
bowing magnificently. "Ah, madame, why did you
leave me when I was on the point—of venturing——"

"You will venture—?" she cried suddenly.

"Anything, madame, for you."

"The sooner the better," she murmured. "This
way—the horses are waiting! The priest is at the
chapel!"

"O Romeo, Romeo!" chuckled the actor, as he followed jauntily.

.   .   .   .   .   .

When some guests passed that way at midnight they
found the Duke lying bound and gagged by the pathway, but wearing his bonds very gaily, with the spirit of
one who had escaped from a heavier bondage. They
unbound and restored him to freedom, but the bonds of
the actor could not be undone, for a minister tied the
knot.

The Master Marksman.

"TUT! tut! Hayhurst! Hayhurst! Hayhurst!" growled the Major, plaintively. "Nothing but Hayhurst! Everybody talking about Hayhurst even yet. It's Hayhurst when I go out, and Hayhurst when I come in, Hayhurst when I stand up, and Hayhurst when I sit down. Flags flying, bugles blowing, drums beating, dogs barking, civilians shouting, all Hayhurst, Hayhurst, Hayhurst. And what has he done, sir? I ask you what has he done? Shot something. And what has he shot?—a target, pshaw!"

"And what would you have him shoot?" asked the bank official (an emigrant from Hamilton) revengefully. "A house?"

"No, sir—a man, a man, a living, real, animate man. An enemy of his country, sir, his queen and his God. To shoot a target—a mere target, a helpless, inanimate, unbiased target! What merit is there in that? But to shoot a man, to shoot him at the right time in a gentlemanly manner and a vital spot, to shoot him with caution, with courtesy and with a Snider bullet, on behalf of your queen, your country and your God, with patriotic devotion, above the belt, so that he will perish and die—that, sir, is the work of a master marksman such as no mountain hamlet can produce. But I have known members of Her Majesty's militia, sir, who have shot men (I mention no names), and what was their reward? Drums? No, sir. Bugles? No, sir. Fireworks? No,

sir. Reduced fares? No, sir. Five hundred dollars?
No, sir. Five dollars? No, sir. Drinks? No, sir; but
scars—scars and obscurity."

The Major leaned back in his chair and groaned significantly and mixed another half-and-half, while his
auditors followed suit in sympathy, with the exception
of the bank official, who, fearful for the reputation of his
native village, took his negus unadulterated and turning
the Major haughtily enquired with a cultured sneer,
to "You are quite a shot yourself, I presume?"

" Look at me eye," said the Major sternly. " Observe
me eye. What is the color of it? Gray-blue, a silverish,
grayish blue. That is the eye of a marksman, sir. Have
you heard of William Tell, the hero saint and mountain-
ous marksman, who shot from the head of his patriotic
progeny an apple on behalf of his queen, his country,
and his God? When for the first time I read this
remarkable episode I rose, rushed to the mirror and for
the first time saw the bluish, silverish, grayish promise
of future greatness in my eye. Then turning to myself
I said in clarion tones, ' McManus, you are predestined
to shoot, but not apples. No, not apples. No, but
men, McManus, men.' The next day I joined the
Queen's Own. As a member of this heroic organization
I soon, on the strength of my eye, gained a continental
reputation as a marksman. Holding targets in scorn, I
impatiently awaited the day when the bugle would sum-
mon me to battle to slaughter the foes of my queen, my
country, and my God. At last the day arrived. Wrap-
ped in peaceful slumber one night at my boarding-house
I heard suddenly the agitation of a knocker, and look-

ing out of the window saw the Colonel of the regiment agitating the knocker and crying in thrilling tones :

" ' McManus, arise. The Fenians are upon us. Report at the drill-shed in the morning.'

"And I arose. In a moment I was standing before the mirror. It was there. Yes, the silverish, bluish, grayish light was there at the crisis. The eye and the hand of the master marksman were at the service of his country. The predestined moment had arrived. Others had shot at targets. McManus would shoot the foes of his native land. The trumpet sounded to battle, and we marched to the front with fearless and intrepid step. Ere many hours had passed, as history has recorded, we found ourselves one dim and dusky day in the presence of the foe—the Irish historic Fenian. Far away as eye could stretch, the hosts of the enemy lay before us in martial array. There they lay, sir ; there they lay, a great green host of furious Fenians. The trumpet sounded. Through the crash and the din of the onset I could hear the blood-curdling yell of the Irish, ' Death to the Sassenach ! ' And I knew in a moment that they had detected my presence in the ranks of my country and doomed me to destruction (being a member of L.O.L. No. 38, as well as of the Q.O.R.). It was a critical moment. In the fore front of the battle I lay in skirmishing order and imminent danger by the side of Sergeant Wilkins. The bullets whistled and whirled around us. Thick clouds of smoke obscured our sight. Through the rattle of the rifles, the shrieks of the wounded, the booming of the cannon, the smoke of the artillery, I gazed with eagle eye, seeking the dead-

liest of my country's foes.   Even as I gazed, the bewildered voice of Sergeant Wilkins murmured in my ear :

"'McManus, which is grass and which is Fenians ?
Both is green.'

"'Trouble me not,' I answered ; 'trouble me not
with details.   I am dissatisfied with our conformation.
Our General is a man of great domestic virtues, but nothing but a master stroke can deliver us from the Irish.'
Snider rifle in my hand I pondered deeply, seeking a
way out of destruction.   The fight grew sterner and
sterner ; the noise grew louder and louder ; the smoke
grew thicker and thicker, and suddenly, through the
roar and the din of the battle, the voice of the General
came to my ears, crying, 'McManus, why don't you
shoot ?'   'General,' I answered, 'I abide me time.'

"The fight went on again.   The bullets whistled and
whirled ; the smoke grew thicker and thicker ; the
artillery thundered and boomed, and suddenly again,
through the din and the turmoil of the conflict, the
agonized voice of the General cried :

"'McManus, why *don't* you shoot ?'

"'General,' I answered, 'I am engaged in thought.'

"The artillery battered and boomed, the rifles rattled
and rang, the Irish hooted and howled, the slaughtered
perished and died, the smoke grew thicker and thicker,
when suddenly through the chaos and confusion of the
conflict the sound of a voice in the last accents of
despair came again to my ears :

"'McManus, *why don't you shoot ?*'

"'General,' I answered, 'I honor your domestic virtues.   Leave me alone.'

"The enemy drew nearer and nearer. They surrounded us. They outflanked us. They environed us; and I saw that unless some master marksman intervened to turn the tide of battle we would be speedily extinguished At this supreme moment a sudden inspiration leaped to my mind. I turned to Sergeant Wilkins and swiftly said :

" ' Point out to me the arch-Fenian. Point out to me the commander in chief, the supreme rebel, the greatest, greenest, loftiest of them all. Point him out and I shall bring this painful episode in the history of my country to a sudden close.'

" As Wilkins turned to answer my question his head suddenly disappeared with a look of the greatest astonishment and was carried on the wings of a cannon-ball to the rear of the army.

"Roused to the highest pitch of indignation at this unseemly interruption to our conversation, I determined to bring the battle to a close. The front rank of the enemy was now within a few yards of ours. Quietly creeping through the bushes I entered their ranks and passed unobserved to the rear, where the commander-in-chief, considering the battle won, was standing at ease and being measured for a crown. Stepping in front of him, I gazed upon him sternly. 'General,' I said——

" ' King Patrick, if ye plase,' he interrupted.

" 'General,' I said, ' look at me eye ! "

" He looked and trembled. 'It's McManus,' he cried.

" I covered him with my Snider rifle. 'General,' I said, ' give the word !'

" ' Retreat, ye devils,' he shrieked, ' McManus has a bead on your general.'

" In a moment all was confusion. The enemy fled, and I found me comrades gathered around to congratu-late me on having saved from tremendous destruction me Queen, me country and me God."

A Midnight Minstrel.

THE light of civilization can burn as well as brighten as the sun that shines can scorch, and there are some who feel its rays like daggers, and writhe amidst the thorns its warmth has nourished ; and there are some who at its zenith, live in utter night doomed by the day to darkness. The sun is responsible for the Sahara. There are deserts as well as gardens, and sighs as well as smiles, and in the very centre and soul of civilization a stately soul has lived a withered life, majestically prolific in its gloom.

One of the most remarkable poems which the mind of the nineteenth century has produced, and one which, if merit be the measure of endurance, is destined to live exalted for many centuries more—is that midnight epic, by James Thomson, "The City of Dreadful Night." This poem is the work of a modern Dante, who had no need to search his imagination for a hell, being fortunate enough to live in London. It is even more fearful than the "Inferno" or "Purgatorio," because it is more real. It is not a creation, but a picture. It is not a phantom of a brooding mind, but it is a crape-clad fact, draped, it may be, with the darkness of a sorrowing mind, shrouded perhaps unduly with the raven imagery of individual grief, but still a fact which many sad eyes have seen, a midnight poem of which several sad stanzas had already been written in the intelligible wrinkles of many stricken brows. The touching language of wrinkles is unfortunately one which society is not at all times anxious to read, and which poets searching for a present popularity are seldom brave enough to record, and so it behooved this poet to do it for them, and this while other rhymsters were sweetly warbling of lilies and roses, of azure clouds, and flowers, and silvery streams, and smiling skies and fair coquettes, he grandly, grimly, sternly did, and so behold "The City of Dreadful Night" rising in gloomy grandeur before the eyes of men, its foundation deeply, firmly laid upon the granite rock of fact ; its massive outlines clearly defined for the centuries ; its mighty shadow falling across the plain of ages. It is a negative argument for Utopia, a powerful pamphlet in the propaganda for social reform, and a new and striking feature in the landscape of the world's imagination. "The City of Dreadful Night" must take its place in the pantheon of imperishable thought, there to live exalted when the reality of which it is the image has been wiped away from earth, and there to be gazed at, wonderingly, by eyes as yet unopen and ages as yet unborn, as a dark reminiscence of the barbaric nineteenth century, and spoken of by lips as yet unsealed as "the picture of a hell, called in the language of the ancients, "City."

It is significantly strange that there should be born of human thought works so dissimilar as this author's "City of Dreadful Night" and that other poem of his namesake, James Thompson, "The Castle of Indolence." One is the smile of genius, the other is its frown ; one is the light of day, the other the light of

the night. One is gilded with sunshine, the other is
shrouded with shadow; and yet both came from citizens of a common civilization; but the eyes of one were
surely on the stars, while the other looked at the earth.
And which is the worthiest? The truth is not always
welcome; a smile is more lovely than a frown, laughter
more melodious than sobs, mirth more harmonious
than misery. And, if this is so, what wonder that
Thompson, the happy, has a throne in the temple of
Fame, while Thomson, the gloomy, is exiled from its
walls. A ragged poet, he wanders around its walls, singing a dirge more musical in its plaintive intensity, in its
vast immensity, than any that are sounding in the exclu-
sive precincts of its perfumed halls. But he is dolorous,
and therefore unpopular; he is veracious and therefore unfashionable; and right well and bitterly he
knows that for a time, at least, none but his fellow-
exiles, his fellow-paupers, his fellow-sharers of the
realm of doubt and death and darkness will listen
to the music of his song. Perhaps, had he sung a
sweeter strain, one falser, but more lovely, the crowd
might have flocked from the temple, seized him, borne
him into its sacred precincts, robed him in garments
rare and rich, and placed him on a throne. Sometimes
to the mind of the poet there came a doubt whether it
would not be wiser, kindlier in him to sing in strains less
gloomy. Why should he paint a mournful picture?
Why add to the burden of human woe the tortured visions of his imagination? Why drag the devil from the
depths, the pauper from the poorhouse, the drunkard
from the ditch, and hold them up before the eyes of

sensitive contemporaries or shuddering posterity ?   Why
exorcise the ghosts and bid the angry gods unveil ? The
poet pauses before the gate of the stately sepulchre to
answer :

" Because a cold rage seizes one at whiles
   To show the bitter, old and wrinkled truth,
Stripped naked from all vesture that beguiles,
    False dreams, false hopes, false masks and modes of
       youth.
Because it gives some sense of power and passion,
In helpless impotence to try and fashion
   Our woe in living words, howe'er uncouth."

This man actually differed from his age and gave the
lie to the majority.   Is it necessary to deviate from ex-
position to biography and inform the reader that his age
ignored him in consequence, that he was crucified upon
the cross of hostile criticism ?   That might be safely
inferred from a general knowledge of the times.   James
Thomson was indeed one of those unfortunate poets
who write in poverty and are paid with pain.   Thus,
when he wrote his master epic, with bitter prescience he
predicted that he would be ignored by his age :

  " If any care for the weak words here written,
  It must be some one desolate, fate-smitten,
  Whose faith and hope are dead or who would die.
     *   *   *   *   *   *   *
  Yet here and there some weary wanderer
  In this same city of tremendous night
  Will understand the speech and feel a stir
  Of fellowship in all disastrous fight."

And then standing in bitter loneliness in the night,
standing with stately head bowed down, among ears that
heard not, eyes that saw not and love that stood afar, in
the great city of tremendous night, with lips that trembled and eyes alight with that rare fire that never fades,
and heart bursting with grief and pain and genius, he
turned from the light to the darkness, he gathered his
fellow-beggars around him, the only audience he had,
the only auditors he cared for; and with outstretched
hands and passionate intensity of grief, he poured forth
the mournful music of his song :

" O sad fraternity do I unfold
   Your dolorous mysteries shrouded from of yore:
Nay, be assured, no secret can be told
   To any who divined it not before."

And so the dark tide of turbulent melody flows with
mighty dirge-like music from his mind, scene on scene,
and verse after verse, unfolding new depths of darkness
and new strains of grief.

There is no greater or more prolific subject for poetic
inspiration than the modern city, with its bewildering
revelation of every form and phase and tint and shade
of human nature, fair and foul. There is man in communion with man, dependent on man, warring with
man and interlaced and interwoven by social shackles,
locks and chains into the intricate complexity of society.
It is not in repose but in conflict that human nature is
fully and truly revealed. Man must be studied, not as
an individual unit, but as a component portion of universal unity. He must be heard as a note in the general

harmony, a strain in the common choir. He must be seen under circumstances in which a thousand varying conditions call forth a thousand varying traits of character, and every chord of his being is touched and quickened into life. Thus he is seen in the city. There all the streams and tides of pleasure, sorrow, grief and passion run and riot, meet and mingle. There necessity breeds the thief, envy the liar, sorrow the saint and adversity the hero. There in mad chaos the tides of being ebb and flow, and crystal waters mingle with the black. Here as in a mighty theatre, vast panorama of human nature is unfolded, the shifting scenes of life appear, each actor steps upon the stage, every depth is sounded, every shallow is seen, and innumerable characters, shades of character and possibilities and capacities of character, are revealed. There are the mighty alternations of life, the palaces and tenements, the boulevards and lanes, the sick and poor, the smile and sigh, the laugh and groan, peace and strife, life and death. There noble weakness battles, sadly failing, and vice grows rich on food of human woe, and there on the runes of wrinkled faces may be read the saddest social problem yet unsolved. The city seemed a wilderness whose myriad soils, some sterile, few fertile, grow few flowers and many weeds ; where daily, hourly, momentarily, the seeds are sown and the bitter harvest of misery reaped. There, written in indelible letters upon the intelligible register of living flesh, may be seen the story of every stage in the evolution from savagery to civilization. The old barbarian is there damned with the double agony of his humiliation and the sight of a civilization he cannot share.

There in endless monotony of toil can be seen that saddest slavery—the subjection of mind to the body, the
homage of the thought to the flesh, the bondage of the
intellect to the stomach. There men are degraded to
slaves or automata. There are the invisible chains that
bind with links more cruel and pains more pitiless than
ever despot fashioned or decreed. There is a hopeless
tyranny of conditions, a bastile of social environment, a
conspiracy of circumstances, which terrorize the impo-
tent victim of their necessity, robbing him of everything
but despair. There in cloud of care and shame of sin
and shadow of an omnipresent gloom, the sable city
stands. It stands like a withered tree on whose gnarled
boughs and mouldered limbs sit songless birds and buds
that never blossom ; within whose fibres, roots and heart
the worms creep, breeding rottenness ; and on its top-
most boughs, perhaps, a few green leaves which draw
their nourishment from the roots, which die of stolen life ;
and from the heart of the gloom, from the very centre
and core of dreariest night a denizen, a black raven singing in the tones of a nightingale, pours forth its miracle
of plaintive song, its melody and music of the night.
How sad it is to think that many more caged birds, now
doomed to be dumb or doleful, to faint and die in the
tainted atmosphere and gloom, will never sing their
songs—the songs unsung, the locked harmonies, the
still-born music, born and buried at once ; the world has
slain its best singers before their mouths were opened.
The silent songsters that haunt the dreary depths might
in a happier atmosphere burst forth into music, and palpitate with love, might fill the world with sovereign

strains, divine and deathless, that would repay a thousand times in the golden coin of song the toil that made
them sing.

The poem is a description of the great city at night.
It is the narrative of one who wandered through its
tangled streets and saw them draped and shrouded in
heavy gloom. But there is something more than the
darkness of nature reflected in the poetic picture, the
darkness of the observing mind is also there. The
gloom that pervades the poem is a double gloom. It
comes in part from without the mind and part from
within. The poet saw the city through the veil of
his despair, which was only intensified by the
kindred gloom of night. To the brooding mind of
Thomson, the city was dark at any time, dark in the
dawn, dark in the day, and doubly dark at night. For
there was darkness in his mind that pondered, and darkness in the eyes that gazed and darkness in the thought
that mourned. His was a grief stricken mind, and he
felt magnetic sympathy with kindred gloom, so fitly
symbolized by brooding night. The ingredients that
enter into the composition of the poem are dual—subjective and objective. The former are permanent, the
latter transitory. The misery of the city may by just
statesmanship be alleviated and destroyed, the problem
of poverty may be solved in time, the light of genius may
dissipate the darkness of the civic bastile, and shed prosperity and peace into the darkest ditches and the saddest slums. Industrial order may supplant industrial
confusion, co-operation may supersede a competition
which has degenerated into robbery and theft. The city

may be cleansed, the stains of vice, crime and poverty, which are born of social inequality and injustice, may vanish with the advent of social equality and content. The city of Dreadful Night, as a present fact and feature of society, may vanish with time, the objective source of the poet's gloom may disappear, but the subjective capacity for grief must remain. There is no alchemy in time to extract the gloom from the mind of man. It is part of the web and woof of human nature. It is the dark thread in the fabric of thought. It is an elemental mood of mind. When the worlds mingled together, and the nebular currents, freighted with cosmic fire, framed and fashioned in mingled ecstasy and agony the tissue of material being, the ingredients of gloom were mingled with the rest.

It has been said that every man has his mission. Let it also be said that every poem has its purpose. I like to think that even the faintest rhyme is not written altogether in vain, but brings its humble strain of melody to the store of universal harmony, its tribute of ideas to the treasury of universal thought, that, behind the magic of its music, and the mystery of its meaning, there lurks the grandeur of its moral,—that it is freighted with a fact, and carries with it in its journey to the realms of individual thought, the divine illumination of a new and welcome truth; that when the master thinker wrought it from the texture of his thought, he fashioned it a soul. It may be that the thought that is the spirit and the essence of a poem is never completely severed from the poet's mind; that though visibly detached, it is invisibly linked to its source, that there are

subtle chords of tenuous thought, and telepathic contin-
uity, which still connect it with the parent mind, and
that, when by sense of sound or sight, another thinker
becomes cognizant of its being, he has but (in the words
he saw or heard) been linked to invisible circuits of
thought and wrought into communion with the creative
mind.   If every poem has its purposes, and every fabric
of fancy its foundations of fact, it may be asked what is
the meaning which lies concealed in the heavy drapery
of this frame ; what are the facts it commemorates, and
what is the measure of its reality?   Psychology would
seem to teach us that every conception is a combination
of perceptions, that the material of thought is supplied
by experience.   If this is so then must these mental
types united in two poems have had these actual prototypes ; ideas were based on images and images cast on
the retina by the external world.   On logical grounds,
therefore, we affirm an external material reality as the
prototype of this internal mental production.   Even if
it were what the plutocratic critic will pronounce it—a
dream, the laws which govern the production and deter-
mine the character of dreams, inexorably declare that
they must find their basic material in the external en-
environment of the mind ; but in the realm of midnight
thought, no stranger ever enters.   The subject matter of
dreams is supplied by experience of waking life.   Com-
binations, exaggerations, grotesque imitations of the ma-
terials of experience, there may be ; but the ideas of
which the mental monstrosities are composed can all, if
analyzed and separated, be traced to the environment of
daily life, and in citizens of dreamland, like the strange

phantoms that throng the mind in delirium, and lineal descendants of the inhabitants of earth, emigrés from the republic of reason to empire of imagination, staid upright thoughts, who take advantage of the night to join a mental masquerade and revel in the Saturnalia of midnight fantasy, and the weightiest authorities on hypnotism inform us that the hypnotist can never discover in the mind of his subject, or unveil any experience not supplied by and limited to the world environment of subject. If this is so, we may safely conclude deductively, that there was an external reality to suggest this poem, and inductive evidence of this fact is furnished by the presence of the city of London itself. Thomson was therefore no "idle singer of an idle day." He was a dealer in facts, a builder with truths. "The City of Dreadful Night" is no chimera of the poetic mind. Poverty no phantom is ; misery, no myth. The fields of the nineteenth century are stained by many cities such as this. Feudalism exiled from the political sphere still reigns in the industrial. Charity is powerless to destroy it, for it does not touch the roots. A symmetrical structure cannot be built on the old foundations.

Pessimism is born of ignorance. There is both pain and misery in the world ; but pain is discord, and discord is evanescent and transitory. It is incomplete and limited in time. Harmony is absolute and universal, because it is complete, and in every mind that perceives discord by its capacity to do so, proves that it has harmony, as by its capacity to know division it manifests its unity. Why did the poet know that pain was pain ? Because it jarred with something which was not pain and which he carried in his mind, because the harmonious within revolted and rebuked the discord without.

What a strange home for genius—that thing of bewildering light—was this dark city. There is no sun or star or satellite, which gives forth light like genius. The primordial elemental cosmic fires burn in the mind of man, and daylight, dawnlight, moonlight, sunlight, starlight, jewel-light, electric light, and even the light of candles on the highest of altars, burn dim in the presence of genius. The rays of thought are cosmic and supernal, they find the way through mists and clouds and nights, and shrouds and doubts; yes, and through the deepest fold of night called death, they find their glorious way—these mystic rays of thought. Why, then, with such fire in his mind, did James Thomson despair? Was his genius too feeble, or was dust too thick to let him see in ecstasy of intuition, as may by some be seen, that only the imperfect can die : that harmony is external, omnipresent, infinite; that thought is the basis of being and made of fair spirit stuff, which only dies to purify its threads ; that mind could not comprehend the relative were it not absolute, the finite were it not infinite.

It is strange of all the world's cities, London should have been chosen as his home, strange that his thoughts should hear groans for cradle song and sighs for lullabys. These things are sadly strange, but the thing sublimely strange is this—that to all the leagued powers of the city whose mission it was to cripple and maim, could neither maim nor dwarf nor cripple the strength and majesty of his mind. The mind expanded even there and broke the chains of hostile circumstances. But there were other cities where it was not darkness. All were not Londons. Even as he sighed, others in happier civic homes were smiling. The world was not wholly miserable. The habitations of all men were not gloomy. Beneath the lights of other skies, other and happier cities had their place, and cherished in their myriad homes the throbbing hearts of millions. Venice the beautiful, caressed by silvery waves, throned on a smiling sea, crowned by a heaven of perpetual light, and kissed and kindled into life and joy by sun and sea and star. Florence the golden—a jewelled picture in an azure frame—a marble memory of greater days when all her palaces were decked with dreams— dreams from the mind of Angelo, dreams from the soul of Leonardo, dreams from the brain of Raphael, and saved from time forever by spiritual threads that lent them deathless life. Lovely Florence, the witchery of art and sky and soul, the music of lutes and lives and loves, the perfumes of perfect flowers, the glory of crowned art all met and mingled there. No wonder the great Dante had to leave her walls to find a hell. Paris was another city of delight, another town that had what London lacked, a city of the Celts, that people in whose breast the God that made them planted the flower of perpetual joy, whose revolutions were sunbursts, whose bloody deeds were blossoms and brought forth flowers, whose battles only seemed to fertilize their soil, who never had to seek delight because they carried it, whose every tear brought forth its rainbow, whose gloom was of the surface, and whose mirth was of the depths, who never fell except to rise again more glorious. There marble fountains toss their waters in the air, and when the stars come out, the murmur of glad voices and silvery laughter mingles with music of harps and violins and lutes, and a thousand stages tremble to the music of the dancer's tread and the songs of the minstrels of joy. San Francisco, throned on the majestic mother of seas—the vast Pacific, looking out through her Golden Gate with loving glance across the dreamy depths, freighted with orange groves, with luscious fruits, and rich with ruby wine, the Mecca of the sick, blessed with perpetual summer, in whose air microbes take wings and fly, peace conquers pain, and men grow rich with joy, and full to satiety with a sensous, somnolent breath of delight.

These were the other cities, but he knew them not. Only one did he know, and that was the greatest, darkest and most terrible of all. A city not of joy, not of peace, not of rest, not of art, not of love, but a "City of Dreadful Night." So he found it, so he painted it, and so he has bequeathed it to the ages. Even after living, London is dead ; it will live again in his verse. He will pass with his dolorous vision down the aisles of many ages. A bard in black, he will unfold his tale to the wondering ears of posterity. He will gather them from their revels in the golden age, and in the midst of their festivity he will speak, and the voice of joy will be hushed. By the witchery of his voice and verse he will awake again the tortured night, and dimly outlined within it they will see the midnight city, faintly, misty;

there will be seen again in the twinkling lights the
gloomy outlines of the dreary houses, the bridge of suicides, the domes of dark cathedrals, the steeples of vanished churches, the leprous lanes, the multiplied beating
of the sea of sobs and sighs, the dark Thames, the beg-
gars, the usurers, the broken images of men, and in the
midst of all, a cowering figure casting a lurid light over
the whole with his eyes, the soul of the city, with head
bowed down, a ragged miserable minstrel, pointing with
withered hands to the charnel pile and sobbing in
dreary, hopeless tones, that weird refrain, ending fear-
fully, breathlessly sad :

"As I came through the city, thus it was
    As I came through the city."

Perhaps posterity, kinder than age, he dragged before
them for judgment, will realize that the crape of his
cloak, the raven sable hue of his thought, the darkness
of his verse did not belong to himself, but that his generation had robed him in black. Perhaps posterity,
looking through the veil he wore, a web so closely spun
by tangled thought, so stained by centre gloom, will see
within as white and pure a soul as ever glorified the
name of man. The truth will not be hid. In him it
found a voice that scorned to lie. It spoke, and he was
its utterance. This voice, majestic as the strong seas,
titanic as the towering hills, which, though it knew no
hills and saw no seas, yet gathered in the vastness of its
utterance, the majesty of both the agony of hills, the
grief of gods.

When even at a distance we contemplate the misery

of those depths, when at a distance of some thousand
miles, we feel and share the shame of a derelict humanity
and bade the misery be, and stretches out no hand to
make it cease, when over the waste of waters there is borne
to our ears in Toronto the sobs of the prisoners in the
desolate city, and before our eyes, in tortured gloom,
there rises a vision of the midnight city, freighted with
agony and canopied with care, we cannot but echo in
no steady tone, the bitter words of him who has made
its gloom immortal and bequeathed the "City of Dreadful Night" and its stricken denizens to eternity.

> "The chambers of the mansions of my heart
> In every one whereof thine image dwells,
> Are black with grief, eternal for thy sake.

> "The inmost oratory of my soul,
> Wherein thou ever dwellest, quick or dead,
> Is black with grief, eternal for thy sake."

We gave this poet sympathy as a miser gives
alms to a beggar ; but posterity will give him glory
as the subject brings gifts to a king. He will stand a
midnight minstrel at the banquet halls of posterity, and
when the cup of ruby joy goes round and others string
their golden harps, and tell the children of the dawn
what their fathers have achieved, he will unfold his
dreary tale and tell what they endured.

A Tale of the Twelfth.

TOLD AT THE CLUB.

"**L**ES Oranges! Les Oranges! a bas les Oranges!"
"Wake up, wake up, Major," growled the bank official nervously, "or if you must howl in your sleep, please don't howl in French."

"French, sir," roared the warrior, leaping suddenly from his seat. "Are they coming upon us? I am prepared." He glared threateningly around him until the sight of the familiar faces recalled him to a sense of his surroundings and he resumed his seat.

It was a hot July afternoon and the sun beat down with merciless vigor on the lawn of the club, where as usual at that hour a company of choice spirits were lounging and smoking and occasionally engaging in a conversation decidedly slow until the sudden exclamation of the dozing warrior concentrated their attention on the portly figure of Major McManus, who now sat erect in his chair gazing solemnly around him with an air of gloom and dejection.

"Is this the twelfth?" he asked at last in hollow tones.

"It is," chorused the company with thrilling unanimity.

The Major groaned.

"Enough!" he said. "Enough! Me doom is sealed. The die is cast. The end draws nigh. The days of McManus are numbered. The son of my father is doomed—doomed!"

For a moment the companions of the dejected warrior gazed at him with an air of mingled consternation and curiosity till suddenly to the mind of each came a recollection of a dreadful rumor which furnished a clue to the excited language.   At various times of recent years it had been reported that the Major was a member of a secret society.   During the greater part of the year this rumor was dormant, but every twelfth of July to the sound of fifes and the beating of drums the rumor revived again, and McManus became a centre of dark suspicions at the club.   On these occasions he wore a look of profound mystery, and when asked the simplest question would look suspiciously at his questioner and smiling darkly answer :

"There are some things which may be revealed, sir, and there are some things which may not be revealed, sir."   ▪

On the glorious Twelfth itself he was transformed and patronized his fellowman.

"We come from the North, sir.   We fought at the Boyne, sir.   The blood of McManus adorns the sod of Erin.   Ye may see it to the present day in the form of grass, sir."

On such occasions as this his fellow clubmen regarded him with awe.   They seemed to see an orange halo round his brow.   In fancy they beheld him presiding over dark and mysterious tribunals and administering the blood-curdling rites of esoteric rituals.   The lawyer felt painfully inferior and the bank official was reputed to have chased an inoffensive goat three miles through the slums hoping to track the creature to its lair and find the lodge rooms of a secret union.

Why was it then that on this anniversary of the Boyne the Major was depressed? Why did he shudder in the seclusion of the club-rooms and murmur, "I am doomed"?

" Doomed," echoed the lawyer.

" Sir, I am tracked," said the Major tragically, " I am dogged. Yes sir, dogged by Jesuits, by Jesuits in disguise, sir."

The Major took another glass and groaned another groan.

" Enough," he said. " Enough, I have been singled out for destruction. The bolt may fall at any moment, but ere I die I will reveal to you and to posterity the cause of my annihilation. I will reveal why I am tracked. A year ago to-day I was in the God-forsaken, priest-ridden village of St. Pierre in le Province of Quebec. Why I was there 'tis not for me to say. There are some things which may be revealed, and there are some things which may not be revealed. Enough to say I was there, and with me was Daniel T. Darby of L. O. L. No. 16. There we were, sir ! There we were ; environed, hemmed in and surrounded by mediæval darkness. But did we falter ? No. When the Twelfth of July dawned on that God-forsaken village it found us at the bar of our host, drinking to the health of William of Glorious Memory. The morning passed without catastrophe, but sitting in the parlor, where we had foregathered to do liquid justice to the occasion, I determined that the greatest event in the history of

mankind shou'd then and there be fittingly commemor-
ated. The waves of superstition beat about us. Priestcraft reared its unblushing front on every side. The
minions of midnight outnumbered us by thousands. In
two hours our train would arrive, but between then and
now lay a historic interval in which to do or die. We
had no drums, no banners, and so profoundly sunk were
the populace in the mire of superstition that not even
a fife could be found. But we were there, sir, and the
occasion was also there. I rose, and walking to the
door of the tavern, looked recklessly around. The day
was dull and misty. The village was sunk in silence
and superstition, and everything looked gloomy, God-
forsaken and forlorn. There was an ominous silence in
the lurid air, such as preceded the massacre of St.
Bartholomew. It was a solemn moment. Should we
cower in the tavern or display ourselves? The spirits
of our fathers bade us display ourselves. We determined to organize a procession and parade the town.
We drank again the health of William of Glorious Memory, and drumless, fifeless, and bannerless as we were,
Daniel T. Darby and myself set forth together on that
perilous journey from which we might never return. We
walked from the tavern to the end of the village, then
turning fearlessly we walked from the end of the village
back to the tavern. The clouds of superstition rolled
around us. The waves of Romanism beat upon our
brows. The mists of mediævalism dimmed our eyes.
The blight of bigotry hung above our heads ; the pes-
tilence of priestcraft dogged our daring footsteps and
through the obscuring mists of doganism we could see

the people glaring at us anxiously. On re-entering the tavern we saw a black-robed figure at the bar. But did we falter? No. Raising my goblet to my lips I said in thrilling tones:

"'I drink to the health of William of Glorious Memory.'

"The priest drew back and trembled. A look of fiendish malignity flashed from his mediæval eye.

"'Les Oranges,' he hissed, and crossing himself ten times he turned and fled.

"'Darby,' I said, 'the enemy are upon us. Prepare to die.' A sudden shriek rang through the lurid air. It was the train. Yet there was hope. We marched to the station. Elated by the prospect of surviving (to serve the cause hereafter), I raised my voice to the high heavens and whistled Boyne Water.

"The village rose and gnashed its teeth. Led by a black-robed figure it rushed to the station, and as we entered the car a thousand hungry voices shrieked:

"'Les Oranges, les Oranges, a bas les Oranges.'

"Which translated means, 'The bloody Orangemen. Murder them, skin them, roast them, paralyze the bloody heretics.' The train steamed away. On the station stood a black-robed figure with a diabolic look of fury in his eyes.

"From that moment my fate was sealed. Jesuits dog me. Thrice have I dreamed that I would die to-day. For many days a strange suspicious looking figure has tracked me through the streets. I have avoided him till now, but soon—Great William—there he is."

A shabby, suspicious-looking person had stolen upon

the lawn and was swiftly approaching the major, who murmured hoarsely :

" I await me doom."

A thrill of horror ran through the crowd. The assassin advanced. Suddenly he drew something from his pocket and thrust it towards the major. Was it a dagger ? No, it was a piece of paper.

" Your whisky bill, major," he said.

The Triumph of Realism.

"SUCH things don't happen," said the editor.
"I think they do," said the author.
"No. The tale is not realistic," said the
editor. "The situation is strained, the characters are unnatural, the pathos is overdone, the accidents are fantastic and pass far beyond the boundaries of the
probable. The climax is not warranted by the antece-
dent circumstances, nor is it natural. Men don't die like
that—they die—"

"Like Little Nell," said the author ironically.

"Not wholly, and yet in a fairly decent and respectable manner and with due regard to the solemnity of
the occasion, and the unlimited possibility beyond. The
tale won't do. It is unnatural."

"What do you want?" asked the author grimly as he
received back the rejected manuscript and returned it
to his pocket. "I am capable of writing anything.
Tell me what you want."

"I want something realistic," said the editor, "realistic and at the same time original and unique. A dram-
atic situation, a striking character, a page from the book
of life, true to nature, faithful to facts, one of live tragic
episodes, realistic and vivid and true."

The editor was young and enthusiastic, a type of the
new man in journalism. He had his ideals and aver-
sions and his heaven-begotten inspirations. He had

also his mission, which was to reclaim literature from its
aridity and make it extremely new.

The author was obviously a hack. He also was young
but not enthusiastic. His clothes were threadbare,
his ambition was lukewarm, his boots were worn at the
heels, his soul was the soul of the cynic, his brain was
the brain of a doubter, and the very material sources of
his inspiration were apparent in the patches on his boots.
And yet behind the wearied indifference of his eyes there
seemed at times to glow a flash of some diviner light
which might have kindled into flames imperishable if
fanned by the breath of some kindlier mother than necessity. Did the editor see it ? Who knows ? There
was a curious gleam in his eyes as he glanced at the
dark intellectual face before him.

"'To write like that one must live," said the author ;
"live and suffer and feel. The essence of realism is experience. We chisel our fancies from facts. But the
age is arid, and cold, prosaic. To write like that one
must taste the bitter-sweet—even the forbidden fruit ;
must thrill with life's raptures of loving and living, for
the tales you want are made not of paper and ink, but
woven out of the skeins of the soul, heart, flesh and
blood."

"Yes, to write it you must live," said the editor
thoughtfully, "and if you write it you live forever."

The office door was closed, and buttoning his coat
tightly around him to shut out the cold draught that
blew in from the street, the author walked slowly down-
stairs and stood for a moment on the steps leading to
the street, gazing dreamily before him into the mist of

white snow which, falling through the gathering twilight, shrouded the figures of the passers by in dim fantastic mist.

"What does he wish me to do?" he muttered wearily. "To murder, or rob or love, or do some desperate thing in order that I may feel the things of which I speak, and know whereof I write, and be realistic? And yet it is true enough. The thoughts I have recorded are only the shadows of thoughts, echoes of earlier voices, spectres of other stories, cinders of extinct fires, cinders and ashes and dust. Yes, the things I have written are colorless, lifeless, passionless things, and from a commercial standpoint apparently worthless. Perhaps it is better so."

And as he stood there in the twilight, surveying with introspective glances the barren vista of the life behind him, he seemed to see as in a glass inverted a vision of the joy he had not known, and to become dimly conscious of a deeper life within him, pointing through paths he dared not dream of to heights he could not see.

.   .   .   .

"A letter for you sir," said the postman.

"Ah, yes—from—" said the editor as he opened the paper and read:

"I am writing a wonderful tale, wonderfully terrible and true. I dare not trust it to the post, and live in perpetual anguish lest robbers break in and steal it. A greater never was written, and it is as fresh as the dawn of the morning, as fair as the sunset in the evening, and as true as the truth which trembles and falls from the

pale white lips of God. I have lived it line by line. It is flesh
of my flesh and blood of my blood; agony and ecstacy
are in it, and the light of setting suns, and the blush of
the sweetest of morning's dawn, and the pathetic dusk of
the saddest of evenings. Come. I am perfectly sane. I
can hear them clapping—the generations to come; and
the lights burn bright on the holiest of altars where they
kneel before me—a god. Come. Dinner at eight."

"A modest man," said the editor, " mad as a march
hare. It will be as good as a circus to see him."

.   .   .   .

"Will he come?" said the watcher wearily, as she
gazed at the dead white thing beside her, spectral and
pale in the twilight.   " The cruel man who sowed desire in the humblest heart in the world. Will he come
and behold his work?"

Three candles burnt by the coffin, and the light of
their pale thin rays shone through the sober twilight
and fell on the eyes of the watcher, and on the ink-
stained lines of the story, and on the cold white face of
the dead.   The room seemed full of memories—memories ashen and pale.   They lurked in the folds of the
curtains and in the worn threads of the carpet and the
soiled pages of the books—the books, sad sentinels on
the verge of the valley of thought, bereft of their old
companions, cowered together and trembled, doubting
the measure of their responsibility for the thing that
was lying there dead.

A step on the pavement outside the door halted ir-
resolute, as though the comer were filled with a spirit
of doubting; it fell on the step, and the shrill bell echo-

ed through the hollows of the house till the depths of silence shuddered at the sacrilege of the sound. Then the watcher rose from the coffin and the light of the holy candles fell on her beautiful face as its sorrow deepened into a faint, sad smile. She passed from the room and closed the door and shut in the corpse and candles, the coffin and the dead, and passed down the stairs with outstretched hand as one welcomes a welcome guest.

"You have come," she murmured softly; " and it was kind of you to come." Slowly she turned and led the way up the stairs into the chamber of death. In the centre stood a table, and the table was set as for a feast. At the foot was a chair for the stranger and on each side of it a glass filled with curiously colored liquid. At the head was another plate, and on it lay a pearl-handled pistol.

The editor sat in the chair at the foot of the table and gazed with startled and wondering eyes at the sorrowful face of the watcher, who had taken her place at the head. The only light in the room come from the candles on the coffin, whose rays, fickle and pale and uncertain, flickered gloomily on the living and the dead.

" You had your doubts," said the watcher.

" You had your doubts as to the realism of his works. To-night he died, and I shall die to bear testimony to the folly of your doubts ; and very shortly now your doubts shall die, or if the things you see and read to-night permit your doubts to live, then you shall die."

The voice was hushed for a moment and silence prevailed again.

" That is arsenic to your right and choral to your left,

and this is a pretty little pistol," said the watcher. "In the hand of the corpse in the coffin is a manuscript ; in the manuscript is a soul—the soul of him who died. Within your reach is the strangest and divinest tale that was ever written by man. Rise and take it and read."

He rose. From the cold white hand he took the tale.

"They will call it romance," he murmured once in fear before he died," said the watcher, " and he sent for you to witness that it was not romance. Do you doubt ? "

" It is true," said the editor, for he saw the tragic truth in her eyes and the truth in the face of the dead.

" Your doubts are dead," said the watcher, "and you may live to say they are dead. And he is dead and I— pass the choral—or I fire ! "

He passed the cup.

" He is immortal as the gods," she murmured, then she drank ; " and I am dead forever."

The candles grew dim in their sockets.

"Go," she said. " The soul—which you bought—take it with you ; the body I love lies here."

Peace and War.*

(SCENE—A mountain in Macedonia. Peace and a Man are standing together and War approaching in the distance.)

MAN—Who is that stranger that is drawing near us,
filling the earth and heaven with brazen clamor, distilling
darkness from his sable wings, awaking ancient fevers in
my blood, and stirring in my soul a dreadful presage of
some illimitable evil?

WAR—I am War—glorious War—come back to the
world again to kindle splendid chaos and destruction
and set the nations one against the other. Long have I
waited in remotest darkness, an exile from the earth, my
ancient kingdom, but now I come again, my ancient
ally, to let your panther passions loose again. Here,
take the glittering sword I bring you and slay the piteous
wretch who stands beside you.

MAN—You are a stranger, yet familiar. Your voice
is thunder and your eyes are lightning, and you have
stirred within me something that was sleeping, but
Peace and I have long been allies also ; I love her well,
and she has made me lovely. We have been happy together, and——

WAR—What! is this little bleating lamb a man?
—this puny little creature who is whining of love, and
peace, and gentleness and mercy—is this my ancient
ally, Man, who used to look so beautiful in battle, and
wade through seas of blood to crowns and sceptres? Is

*Written on outbreak of war between Greece and Turkey.

this the purple-blooded ruler of creation, whose war
songs filled the universe with music and sent the lesser
creatures cowering to the lair, who fought his way from
savagery and weakness up to possession and supreme
omniscience? If Peace had preached to you when
you were hungry, you would have died of that
starvation which is the fate of those whose lands you
conquered.   Here, take again the glittering sword I give
you.

PEACE—The flowers are budding, and blushing and
blooming on the battle-fields of old.   Men have forgot
their ancient enmities and called each other "brother"
for a time.   The golden grain is ripening in the fields.
Deep in the graves the ancient wrongs are buried.   The
evil sores are healed, and gentle music comes from the
harvest fields where truth is ripening and men and maids
are singing songs of joy and reaping rich fruition of co-
hesion.   The voice of war was hushed, and in the little
cottage in the valley—gladly forgetful and divinely
happy—the mother tells her heart that peace is sweet.
Sweet is the song the mother sings, and sweeter than
the breath of flowers budding——

WAR—And Man, the ancient ruler of creation, whose
sword flashed like a flaming brand in battle, has cast
aside the symbol of his greatness and lain down among
the cows and sheep.   The eagle has become a cooing
dove, and the red blood has turned to milk and water.

MAN—Give me the sword.   I was a tiger once, and
fought the other brutes and conquered them, and when
you speak the tiger wakes again and cries aloud for
blood, beautiful blood! blood! blood!

PEACE—What, will you leave me? I, who made you holy; I, who lifted you above creation and made you poet, painter, statesman, thinker; I, who called forth the music of your soul and placed the jewelled crown of civilization on the forehead of the brute; I, who have nurtured, fondled, made you kin to angels? What can you give to me—

MAN—I give you this! (*Stabs her.*)

One Chum

"GOOD-BY."

The warm hands clung together quivering and loth to part, and the dark eyes looked into the grey eyes till the grey eyes faltered and fell, and the trembling lips of their owner whispered :

"Don't take it so hard, old man."

"O, Billy, how could you?"

"Nonsense—this—this marriage needn't make any difference—we can still be friends, you know. There is only a woman between us."

"Only a woman."

"One would think I was going to a burial instead of a wedding," said his companion nervously, with his eyes still cast on the ground.

"Many a man has buried a friend when he married a wife," muttered the other gloomily, and his eyes glanced broodingly back to the day when a thousand hopes were buried beneath the burden of this great treason. They had been so happy up in the old attic room where they had kept batch together—he and Billy. Through a mist of tears he seemed to see again the happy days gone by—the old school-room where they had sat as boys—the cricket field where they had played —the river where they rowed—and all their early griefs and joys rose up before him—the sorrows and the joys they had shared together.

"She is so pretty, you know," the apologetic voice of

his companion broke in upon his thoughts, "and—and —she has n.oney and—Jack, why don't you speak?"

The old school bell was ringing in his ears. He heard again the voices of the boys. His soul was haunted by a vision of green fields and happy voices. "Played, sir! Played! Tackle him low, Billy!" Where was it? The memories crowded upon him with a rush of sweet remembrance—the old school-house, the merry games and the days of auld lang syne.

"It will start me in business, you know," continued the faltering voice of his companion, "and besides— besides—a man must get married some day, you know— and besides, it needn't interfere with our friendship, and for God's sake say something, old man—say something."

They had been so merry together up in the old attic room. He played the old fiddle and Bill smoked the old pipe, and they read the poets together, and the boys came in to see them, and he had thought—had thought——

"Jack speak to me—say something. Jack! Jacky— if you wish—do you wish—Ah, here comes Mary. Let me introduce you to—O, Jack!"

He shrank back and trembled, for his eye uplifted had met the eye of his companion and he cowered before its fire—its scorn. Another moment and his hand was cast aside. Strong arms were thrown around him.

"Here's one for auld lang syne," cried Jack, wildly, as he clasped him for a moment to his heart, then cast him fiercely from him at her feet.

" Traitor, begone with your woman ! "

.   .   .   .   .   .

" What's the matter with the old fiddle ? Nothing
but discord, discord, discord."

He threw the instrument petulantly on the table,
muttering, " It seems all out of tune—since—Billy—
went away. He used to sit there in the arm-chair and
say ' Bravo !' when I played—but now—— Pshaw !
this cursed pipe won't draw. Ah, here's another—
Billy's ; his wife won't let him smoke, and he left it here
for me. To hell with it ! "

He cast it into the fire and grimly watched it burning,
then suddenly plunged his hand into the flames and pulled
it out again and laid it lovingly on the table, feeling a
fierce spiritual joy in the physical pain of the burn.

" I pulled you out of the fire and I pulled him out of
the water, and I would have gone through hell fire to
make him happy, and now———"

He buried his face in his hands.

.   .   .   .   .   .

" What a rude fellow that old chum of yours was ! I
wonder you could associate with fellows like that, Willie
dear. You must cut those old friends and stay at home
with your wifie. Won't you, Willie dearie ? "

She laid her head lovingly on his shoulder and kissed
him on the cheek, but he thrust her aside.

" Go on with your novel, you little fool, and leave my
friends alone."

" What an old bear it is, to be sure," she said pout-
ingly; but keenly alive to the fact that nothing but con-

ciliatory methods would accomplish the immediate object she had in view she continued her caresses.

"Now, ducky, don't oo be naughty to oo little wifey, but treat oo little Mary with——"

"For heaven's sake, what do you want, woman?" groaned Billy wearily. "Is it a new bonnet or a ticket for the concert?"

"Well, you know, dearie, I haven't been to the theatre for two nights, and you promised——"

"Very well, I will take you," cried her husband impatiently, and she bounded triumphantly away to the ·mirror and left him alone in the room gazing dreamily at the fire, glad to be freed from her presence, but bowed beneath the burden of a memory which would not vanish while life remained. His heart felt very lonely as he thought of the vanished days and the great heart he had cast aside to win this flimsy woman. What was the silly chatter of this shallow woman compared with the wit, the pathos, the sweet familiar tones of that most eloquent voice which had spoken to him so often in the little attic room above the trees? What consolation had matrimony to offer him for the loss of that sweet companionship and those noctes ambrozianæ, those splendid vanished nights when the fires of wit burnt brightly in the little attic room where he and Jack had laughed and talked together, and planned, and dreamed, and played the old fiddle, and read the great books, and dreamt the great dreams, and built such splendid castles in the air together? That merry music, that dear voice, those flashing eyes, and that great loyal heart beating in time to his—he would never know again.

Since the day they had parted he had heard nothing of
Jack, and dared not write him, for he knew the friend he
had lost would take no tainted love.

"I must go home to mother at once, Willie," said a
shrill voice behind him, as his wife bounded breathlessly
into the room. "The smallpox is in the neighborhood
and it is really dangerous to stay, and—gracious—how
pale you look, I believe you are getting it. Heavens, is
that the bell?"

She dashed hurriedly from the room and soon he
heard the sound of carriage wheels, and the servants
who came to carry him to bed brought a neat little perfumed note.

"DEAR WILLIE,
                    I will send the doctor at once. You
have the symptoms of smallpox and I will stay at
mother's till you recover, for even if it doesn't kill one,
you know, it ruins one's complexion. Good-bye, dearie."

"Thank God," he said, "thank God."

  .   .   .   .   .   .

This was the worst case the neighborhood had known,
and long the patient tossed upon his bed and in his
mad deliriums talked of footballs, and schools, and
cricket fields, and "Jack." This was the name forever
on his lips, and until the day when all the servants had
fled from the house in horror from the fell disease, a
stranger arrived at the house and took his place by
the bed.

  .   .   .   .   .   .

The patient had recovered and stood by the bed of
his nurse one cold grey evening as the twilight was

melting into night. The sick man was slightly delirious and wandered in his speech.

" Listen to the bell," he muttered dreamily. " Do you hear the school bell, Billy ? Hustle, or we'll be late."

" Hush, Jack," sobbed his companion. " Keep up your heart and get well."

" My heart," cried the sick man wildly, " I haven't got any heart. I gave it away to Billy and he squeezed it like a lemon and tore it to pieces and jumped on it. O, Billy ! "

" No, I didn't, Jack. I loved you—always—see I am Billy—the Billy you nursed back to life."

" Billy is dead," said the sick man sadly. " He died at a wedding."

The voice grew weaker and weaker and night and death drew nigh. Suddenly the shadow of delirium passed from the tired face and the bright eyes opened feebly, gazing wistfully around.

" I am going to heaven," he muttered; " I wonder will Billy be there."

" Here, Jack, here ! " sobbed his companion, bending eagerly above him, filled with a passionate craving for one last word of love.

The eyes beneath him flashed suddenly with a look of divinest recollection—divinest forgiveness—and the pallid lips were parted with the same sweet smile of old. Then the face was thoughtful a moment.

" There are no marriages in heaven," muttered the patient gladly. " We will keep bach in heaven, Billy— you and I. I'll play the old fiddle and you'll smoke the old pipe."

A smile of supreme contentment passed over the worn face.

" Good-bye, Billy."

" Good-bye, Jack."

The warm hand clung to the cold hand quivering, and loth to part, then dead eyes looked into the grey eyes and the grey eyes faltered and fell.

A Master of Intrigue.

THERE is a subtle element in history which priests call providence and fools fatality, but which is neither providence nor fate but only human genius veiled. Behind the play of passions and the war of words there lurks the brooding presence of ambition and thought concealed forms life revealed after the pattern of its dark desires. Dark are the depths of the Tiber and red the recesses of the Seine, but darker and ruddier still are the depths of the realm unrevealed, within whose sombre shades and winding paths reign the masters of unwritten arts, who pull the strings that set the little puppets going upon the mimic stage of history.

" We who make history cannot write it," said Metternich, but he might more fittingly have said, " We who make history *dare* not write it." For there are things behind the things we see, deeds delicately done and tragic tales untold, and ever through the hallows of the ages there comes the muffled sob of candour crucified, and the light laugh of the duplicity crowned ; and perhaps it may be well to deviate a little from the trodden pathways of tradition, and, leaving the orthodox historian in weighty consideration of the dust and ashes, the rags and ruins of the past, seek for the living cause behind these casual consequences ; and following to its sources in the individual mind that elusive, causal element which originates events, study in Talleyrand a type of the personal element in history—the "iron hand within the velvet glove," which with such quiet, subtle strength has fashioned the framework of society, woven the network of conspiracy, and sprung the mine of historical catastrophe.

In Talleyrand we see the greatest modern representative of that class of politicians of whom Machiavelli was the interpreter and Guicciardini the historian, but whose representatives are older by far than the worthy sages of Florence, and whose lineage, if traced to its remotest sources, would carry us back perhaps to that distant day when primeval man amid Cainazoic rocks mated his wit with the cunning of the wolf or matched his ingenuity with the wiles of the serpent in the stern struggle for existence. Nor have the descendants of the primeval parent been altogether unworthy of his fame, and if, from his cave among the pliocene rocks where he had mocked the futile strategy of the baser brutes and utilized his proficiency in perfidy to perpetuate the race, he could have looked forward through the ages and beheld the long line of his progenitors who carried the vulpine instinct to perfection, his soul perhaps would swell with as much pride as ours is sad with shame when he contemplated the innumerable statesmen, priests and princes who crept to power along the winding paths of perfidy, and grew fat on a diet of duplicity. This is not the highest form of genius, but it is apparently the most successful, for it seems to be the peculiar will of Providence that knaves should have the making of history while the hero and heretic find abundant reward in the prison, the scaffold, the crucifix, the stake, the inquisition and the grave. And the masses of mankind, everlastingly duped, have they not fashioned thrones and palaces for the schemer? And weak of knee and blind of eye cowered trembling beneath the lash of their master crying at every fresh infliction, " It is the will of God," running frantically to their priest, their astrologer, their talisman for consolation, while behind the curtain of events, with busy brain and scornful smile, sit the knaves who feed on their folly.

The highest genius is creative. It adds to the sum of human wisdom or human happiness. It touches into music the chords of the soul of man and with fingers of fire, in letters of light, writes deep upon the human consciousness a truth eternal. The thinker —the poet, the statesman, the scientist, the fathers of thought and the founders of nations—these are the beacon lights, the suns of the universe of thought. After them, and on a lower plane, come the men whose light shines not for humanity, but as a dark lantern to guide their individual steps to power. Of such was Talleyrand. He was not the highest type of man. No! very far from that. Many a stately head was laid on the hard pillow of the guillotine, which even lying lowly there did tower above his own. And many a noble soul passed from that tragic stage weary and willing into the shadowland far more heroic than he. For this is the pathos of history that they who sow so rarely reap; they lead the forlorn hope, they scale the heights, they conquer, but they die ; and when they fall, in rush with stealthy tread the birds of prey, the vampires and vultures of history—the Robespierres, Talleyrands, Fouches—and seize the spoils so dearly

bought. But when these men die, they die; while the
grave of a Rousseau, a Voltaire, or a Danton is the portico
to immortality, and their coffin a triumphal car that passes
down the aisles of many ages well welcomed and well
loved.

.   .   .   .

A rustle of silk and a glitter of gold, and the old
court stands before us. There are the pretty puppets
dancing on the crust of the volcano, while underneath,
with restless fury, rage the titanic forces of the
avenging revolution. And over it all with smile and
sneer the heirs of wealth and folly meet and mingle.
Perfumed, powdered, and polished, cultured, courtly
and caustic, in gorgeous silks and glittering jewels,
prince and peer and lord and lady, stately age and
smiling youth, radiant beauty and ready wit, courtier,
soldier, noble and prince, moved through the palace and
banquet halls, bowing and smiling, flirting and joking,
with the polished grace of the vanished days, and in their
midst Talleyrand, Perigord, Bishop of Autun, witty with
the witty, and wise with the wise, holy with the holy,
haughty with the haughty, frailer than the frailest,
stronger than the strongest, and deeper than the deepest,—famous for his *bon mots* and delicate sarcasm,
studying with amused interest the eccentricities of his
fellows, delicately dissecting the motives of rulers, join-
ing in the little intrigues of the court as he would a game
of euchre, and all the time stealthily politely elbowing
his way with courtly grace to power. With delicate
skill he estimated the relative strength and weakness
of his rivals, with cool deliberation he studied the

play of princely passions, and with ceaseless vigilance he followed the ebb and flow of popular emotions. Causes, sources, seeds, these were the things he sought, that he might lay his finger on the springs of action and fashion effects.

.   .   .   .

Why did he not exert his talent to avert the revolution?   The answer to this is simple—because his ability, unlike that of the royal advisers, amounted to genius, and in its light he saw that the revolution was inevitable, that it was born in the cruel past, that it was the offspring of ages, the child of the centuries, the nursling of time, too strong, too vast, and above all, too just to be averted by the art of man.   And even if the people could have borne their burdens a generation longer, and if it had been possible for Talleyrand to creep into the councils of the court and suggest some profound expedient to avert the approaching catastrophe, it is very doubtful if he desired to do so.   Perhaps he was as anxious for a conflict as the mob themselves, for the crisis is the festival of genius.   It is then the voice of necessity calls him and the door of opportunity is open. Then in the conflict of its guardians he can sweep down like an eagle and carry the crown away.   To create a crisis, this is the ambition that has haunted the Richelieus, the Cromwells, the Mazarins, and Borgais. In times of peace the king can dispense with his ministers and play with his fool.   But in an emergency the genius is inevitable.

Nevertheless it is possible that Talleyrand, like many others, was largely influenced in his early attitude toward

the revolution by a consideration of the earlier disturb-
ence of the Fronde, and he may for a time have aspired
to play the role of a Mazarin in the new revolution.

    .   .   .   .   .   .

If such an ambition ever crossed his mind it was not
of long duration, and a careful study of his conduct
previous to 1793 will show that any ambition which he
might have entertained to assume the attitude of a Mazarin
had been by then abandoned. If he failed to obtain
an ascendency over the queen we must ascribe the failure
to one of two reasons, either that Marie Antoinette had
rejected his advances as personal adviser, or that he had
voluntarily abandoned his early intrigues for the control
of the councils of the court, or that in his anxiety to con-
ciliate the people he had gone so far as to excite the
suspicion of the court and thus nullified the effect of his
previous intrigue.   The latter we assume to be the true
explanation of the problem.   It is not at all likely that
had he directed his efforts solely to obtaining a personal
ascendency over the king or queen he would have
failed.   On the other hand, it is difficult to suppose that
though he might relax he would entirely abandon his attempts to control the councils of the court, for it was not
by any means his habit to burn his bridges behind him.
It is therefore likely, as I have suggested in the third
explanation, that if his defection to the popular party
was due to the fact that in his well-founded conviction
that that party was the stronger, he carried his early
advances to its leaders so far as to offend the queen for
whose exceptional susceptibility to suspicion he had
neglected to make due allowance, and seeing at last that

he had lost the confidence of the court he boldly and finally embraced the popular cause. There can not be the slightest doubt, however, that Talleyrand made no perceptible advances to the leaders of the people or even to Mirabeau until he had very thoroughly convinced himself that the royal cause was hopeless, and his foresight and sagacity in his perceiving this at so early a date forms a very striking contrast to the folly of the sovereigns who ignored it.

The student of history who, mystified by the attitude of Talleyrand at this epoch, seeks for a clue in the attitude of his historic prototypes under apparently analogous circumstances, or founds an explanation of his conduct on purely historic data, is liable to form a very erroneous conception of the tendencies of that profound and consummate mental strategy which governed his actions and determined his attitude to the court and revolution. There was an element present in the environment and in the calculations of Talleyrand peculiar to the time and land in which he lived, though of comparatively no interest to Ximines, Richelieu, Alberoni or other past masters of the art of intrigue. This was the element liberated by the revolution—the will of the people. If Talleyrand was the last of the courtiers he was the first of the politicians. He marks a critical stage in the evolution of the demagogue, the stage when the courtier develops into the politician and the suppliant for princely favor becomes the suppliant for the suffrages of the people. It is true the masses existed physically before the revolution, but their political existence had been largely potential till then. Hitherto they had been

subject to the sovereign, and the courtier who won the
favor of the prince could generally control the country.
The single apparent exception to this occurred at the
time of the Fronde, but those who are familiar with
the secret history of that disturbance will know that the
momentary self-assertion of the people had its origin
largely in the intrigues of De Retz and Mole and never of
itself acquired sufficient importance to be a determining
factor in the conduct of Mazarin, or even of its promoters.   In the time of Talleyrand, however, it became
necessary for the aspirant for office to study not only
the whims of princes but the passions of the people.
The first to perceive this was Mirabeau, who en-
deavored to serve the people in public and the court
in secret, and between them would have fallen had he
lived, for the experiment was too new and popular
passions too high to then admit of the compromise sub-
sequently adopted by Louis Phillipe.   Talleyrand
played the dual role of diplomat and politician.   As the
former he appealed for the favor of princes, as the latter
for the favor of peoples.   In one capacity he sought
the strongest man, in the other the most popular
prejudice.   These he always supported till they became
unpopular, then chose the new favorite. If the man was
strong and the idea weak he remained courtier and
served the man.   This is the key to his relation to
Napoleon.   If the idea were the stronger and the ruler
weak he became politician and served the idea.   This
is the key to his attitude to the revolution, and after the
restoration, when realizing that democracy was stronger
than Louis he delicately reconciled the functions of

courtier and politician as advocate of constitutioned
monarchy.

. . . . . .

And when the crisis came—the mightiest crisis that
France had ever known, the petty politicians quickly
found that the waters of a deluge are not navigable by
those who learned to sail on shallow streams. In the
face of this vast emergency when in the whirlwind of
unique events and clash of titanic passions the ancient
arts of intrigue were confounded, even Talleyrand was
for a time appalled. Of what value were calculation,
inference, induction, or theory of probabilities regarding
the consequences of events which had their origin in
impulse and were subject to momentary modification
originating as in wayward whims or wishes of the mob?
Again the remarkable prescience which had preserved
Talleyrand from destruction on the fall of the throne
preserved him again from the menace of the Terror.
He quietly left the country and went to England, leaving
the factions to destroy each other, while he, preserving
secret communication with all parties, awaited in safety
the result. The sagacity of this move was justified by
events. After a short visit to America he returned
again to France and began that elaborate series of
intrigues which determined his relation to the consulate
and to Napoleon.

. . . . . .

Out of the wreck of the Empire he emerged apparently
triumphant, but his prestige was irreparably damaged. He
had betrayed too great a god to receive the homage of
mankind   The brevity of his premiership at the restor-

ation indicates the universal distrust with which he was regarded by all parties. Nevertheless, on the fruits of his former peculations he lived a prosperous life for many years and lingered long—a stately reminiscence of a tragic past in the midst of a new generation. And what a past it had been ! He had spoken with Voltaire. He had known Rousseau. He had bowed to Louis XV. He had knelt to Louis XVI. He had kissed the fingers of Marie Antoinette. He had seen the most depraved of monarchs and the most detestable of demagogues. He had known the greatest orator, the greatest soldier, the greatest thinker, the stateliest courtier, the greatest fool, the greatest villain, the greatest sovereign, and the greatest republican, in the history of France ; and he had witnessed the greatest event in the history of Europe. He had administered the sacrament in Notre Dame. He had been the idol of the court and the president of the revolutionary assembly. He had made innumerable fortunes, contrived a thousand conspiracies, outlived the boundaries of nations, determined the destinies of kings, stolen the liberties of peoples, and held the fate of empires in the hollow of his hand. And through this wonderful panorama of events, emerging triumphant in court, and cloisters, cabinet, at banquet and council, in salon or parliament, at balls or revolutions, he moved with the same calm, courtly grace as when he bowed to kiss the hand of Louis in the days of the ancient régime. His life was the triumph of treason.

As his long life drew to an end he determined to die decorously. At the last moment the dignitaries of the church and court and the king himself were summoned and knelt by his side, and with them came others, kings who did not kneel, who were not summoned, whom they did not see.

. . . . . .

"But he could not hear the word death without changing color," says his biographer. "His domestics scarcely dared place before him letters sealed with black," and when he lay upon his bed in the last illness his mind dwelt continually in the past. In the long watches of the night, tossing restlessly in his bed, he murmured the names of Louis, Mirabeau, Napoleon, Fouche, Lafayette, and his mind went back to the vanished days and lingered fondly in the salons of the ancient régime where, a golden-haired oracle in silver and silk, he laughed and joked and gambled long ago. And he saw again the gilded butterflies that fluttered round a queenly form, careless, beautiful and gay, and wandering lightly from group to group he heard the merry laugh of Artois, the cultured sneer of Provence, the haughty voice of Montmorency, the courtly tones of Lafayette, and as the music throbbed on the perfumed air he heard outside the marble halls the murmur of a mighty storm, and while within in pride of blood sovereigns and lords and courtiers gaily glided.

"Yet behind all—lowering, cowering—lo, a shape,
Vague as the night, draped interminably, head fast and
    form in scarlet folds,
Whose face and eyes none may see
Out of its robes only this—the red robe lifted by the
    arm,

One finger crooked pointed high on the top like the
head of a snake appears.

.   .   .   .   .   .

" Suddenly out of its stale and drowsy lair, the lair of
slaves,
Like lightning it leaped forth, half startled at itself,
Its feet upon the ashes and rags—its hands tight to the
throats of kings."

The vision of the court had vanished, and he heard
the knocking, fierce, turbulent knocking at the doors of
the bastile, the clamoring and the knocking, and the
voices, mad turbulent voices, silent for centuries, now
aroused, shrieking, cursing, reviling, calling aloud for
bread, for justice, for revenge, thunder of Mirabeau,
thunder of Verginaud, thunder of Danton; and behind
these gaunt figures, the faces, fierce hungry faces writ
deep with passions and pain, while out of the soul's
dark places the panther passions leapt, and liberty,
bloody but beautiful, arose, unchained and unforgiving.
What were those pale figures that were hurried forward
amidst the chaos, confusion, derision, in faded tinsel and
silk, trembling and weak up to the bloody guillotine—
king and queen and courtier—the gay old court now
bleeding, helpless, headless, all—all except Citizen Talleyrand, ex-bishop of Autun, most estimable revolutionist.
Turbulent voices and bloody faces, fury and fire and
fear, sons of the Terror, remembering, reproaching, re-
venging with fire and steel and lead, and lo ! in the
midst of it all, over it all, prevailed the music of the
marseillaise, the sound of the nations arising, the tramp

of approaching armies, the call of the stricken republic, the bugle, the smoke and the thunder, the clash of opposing armies, the rattle of musketry, the shrieks of the wounded, the smoke of the battle-field, the clash of steel to steel, battle and blood and death, and out of it all emerging the spirit of war incarnate in Napoleon, a meteoric star, glittering and dazzling and flaming, daring, dazzling, deluding, hushing contention and crushing freedom, then over the land subdued out of the breathless silence the sound of a silvery trumpet thrilling, daring the nations to battle. The clash of contending armies, the drums, the bugles, and banners, the eagles triumphant and haughty, the sun of Austerlitz arising, the chorus of exultant soldiers through the smoke and the turmoil arising "Vive le Empereur!" Veterans of Valmy and Arcola, veterans of Jena and Friedland, veterans of Marengo and Bordino, decked with the legion of honor, wounded and scarred and battered, how proudly and lovingly they shouted "Vive le Empereur!" Reproachfully they watched him, haunting him who summoned the hostile armies against the chief they bled for, and then he saw the last great horror and the end. Hand-in-hand, a little time upon the hill-tops they had wandered, Napoleon and Nemesis (ex-bishop of Autun). Then he beckoned to the nations and lo, the empire fell—and now—how they crowded round him in the midnight—ghosts from the guillotine, ghosts from the battle-fields and a grim ghost from St. Helena. The visions and the voices, aye the voices, soft courtly voices murmuring "Vive le Roi," fierce, hungry voices shrieking "Vive le Revolution!" rough soldier voices shouting "Vive le Empereur!" For he had known them all, yes and had echoed them all, ay and betrayed them all, and now they all awaited his coming beyond the ghastly gates. And so with his ghosts around him he passed from the presence of men. Forever from the presence of men—a prince in his own generation—a handful of dust to posterity.

Toronto, 1894.

Love and Pride.

Ah ! love, I am strong and you are frail,
    Or you are strong and I am frail, maybe ;
Let one be frail, let one prevail,
Ere from the night the tremendous gale
    Sweep both into the sea.

A Rebel.

THE king came out of the palace and stood by the marble steps dreamily watching the moon. A cloak of scarlet and velvet hung over his slender frame, and his white hand rested carelessly on the jewelled hilt of his sword. His royal face was clouded by very human care and the sovereignty slept in his eyes. A mighty poor specimen of a king he seemed to me, who had lately come to the court with a royal ideal in my mind, and had lingered on the terrace to compare the dream with the man. Alas! was this moon-struck, love-sick swain a king—a ruler of men? In a moment he turned his eyes from the moon and fixed them on my face, then suddenly flushed scarlet.

"You are pitying me," he cried. "How dare you pity a king?"

Here was a pretty pickle. I had just arrived at court seeking preferment, and now by a careless glance I had made a foe of the king. Where truth is treason silence is safety, and so I stood silent before him.

"You carry your head rather high for one who is only a page," he cried, with an angry stamp of his foot. "A touch of an axe on the neck might humble your pride a bit."

This was too much for my patience. King or no king, his language outdistanced discretion and kindled sudden fire in my heart. I laid my hand on my sword.

"If you were not a king——" I said.

"What then, my pretty spark?"

"Why, then you would be a corpse," I answered hotly.

He stared at me a moment, then suddenly burst out laughing.

"You are the funniest courtier I have ever met," he said. "And why do you pity me, pray?"

"Oh, you are only half a king," I answered warmly, for his laughter touched my pride. "I have read about kings in books, but you are not like a king."

"And I have read about courtiers in books," he answered lightly, "and you are certainly not like a courtier. But wherein am I short of perfection?"

"Oh, you are moon-struck," I answered recklessly. "Look at you idling and dallying here at the beck and call of a woman when your kingdom is going to ruin and traitors are seeking your throne. A pretty sort of a king to be running after petticoats when there's fighting to be done."

"Whom do you want me to fight?" he muttered in a bewildered tone of voice.

"Fight yourself," I answered scornfully, "and slay the slave within you. Shake yourself loose of the shallow sex. They are frivolous jades, I assure you, and not at all to be trusted. If you must love, love someone who can kindle a king within you, and not a moon-struck swain."

"This language is strong," he answered watching me with a strange light in his eyes. "Pray, is your sword as sharp as your words?"

"Try it," I answered briefly.

"I will," replied he quickly. "I have never met

one of your kind before. I will put your bravery to test."

He paused for a moment thoughtfully, then pointed his finger to a pavilion half-hidden among the trees in the park before the palace.

"In a couple of hours," he said, "be there, where a champion of the king will meet you and put your courage to test."

I bowed, and he turned away and re-entered the door of the palace. I passed along up the terrace, intending to descend, when a door at the farther end suddenly opened and a woman came slowly out and dreamily looked at the moon. I don't take much interest in women, but the conqueror of the king had a certain interest for me, and I stood for a moment watching her, feeling considerable wonder to think that so shallow a creature could bring a king to her feet. Suddenly she turned and faced me with an angry toss of the head.

"You scorn me," she said haughtily; "how dare you scorn a queen?"

It is time enough to be bullied when one is married, but women are very conceited and need to be carefully handled, and her lofty tone, so irritating to my pride, was possibly due to a mistake.

"Madame," I answered warmly, "the shadows have deceived you, and I am not the king."

"That is easily seen," she muttered wonderingly, "but who on earth are you?"

"I am a freeman," I answered loftily.

"A little too free," she answered saucily, "and somewhat forward for a boy."

"If you were not the queen——" I muttered, stung to the quick by her sneer.

"What then, my saucy rebel?"

"Why, then you would be a slave," I answered, and she suddenly dropped her eyes.

"Is your heart as brave as your eyes?" she murmured.

"Try it," I answered proudly.

"I will," replied she quickly. "I will choose a champion to test it, in a couple of hours, at, say, that quiet pavilion there among the trees, and if you conquer I will forgive you."

We bowed to each other gracefully and she quietly turned away and re-entered the palace door. Now, here was a pretty predicament. I suddenly recollected that by an unfortunate coincidence she had named the very place and hour selected by the king. Well, what did it matter? I have a relish for swordplay, and have pinked a couple of men before to-day. I could take them on both at once—the more the merrier, for what's the use of living if one can't have a little fun with whatever comes along?

The moon had hidden behind a cloud when the eventful hour arrived, and I found the park decidedly dark as I picked my way through the trees in the direction of the pavilion appointed for a rendezvous. A lonelier place for a meeting it would have been difficult to select, for though in the royal park, the use of the place was forbidden to all but the family of the king, and its seclusion from the world was absolute.

Picking my way through the bushes, I walked along

the soft grass to what was apparently the back of the pavilion, then suddenly paused, for standing face to face in the centre I saw a couple of shadows enveloped in cloaks and eying each other cautiously. Then one shadow spoke softly in a voice that was strangely muffled :

" Rebel, I am the champion of the Queen. Why did you scorn the Queen ? "

And the other :

" Rebel, I am the champion of the King. Why did you pity the King ? "

Then the shadows removed their masks, and a King and a Rebel stood facing each other, but I was not the rebel.

Toronto, Jan., '98.

Sweet Marie.

HE threw the book aside, and rising restlessly from his seat paced impatiently to and fro in the narrow limits of his attic room.

"Who can beat that?" he muttered feverishly. "The light of stars and the perfume of flowers are in it."

Who could he be, this rival who had won the affections of the public, whose name was on every lip, whose book sold like wildfire, while he, poor devil, sat starving in his little attic, feeding on dreams and in momentary expectation of a visit from his landlady for arrears of rent? Why had fame passed him by to visit the domicile of his rival? It was hard—very hard. He picked up the paper again and glanced at the advertisement—ah! there he was again:

"The Queen of Scots, a tragedy in three acts, by Eugene Morell, will be performed to-night at the Theatre Francais. Mlle. Marie Roselli will play in the title role—Mary of Scots. The performance of this, the first drama of the talented young author, is looked forward to with much interest. Monsieur Morell is singularly fortunate in securing the services of the beautiful Marie Roselli to create the character of the Queen."

He dropped the paper with a groan. "So," he said, "Marie—She, too, will contribute to his glory. It was not enough that he should win the affections of the public—ah! that was very hard—but he wrote a play, as I write plays, but his are of course accepted, and she, of all others will play them."

This was the unkindest cut of all. Had he not scrap-
ed and saved, time and again, out of his meagre earn-
ings to keep enough to enable him to indulge in the one
luxury of his lonely life, a seat in the top gallery of the
theatre? And from there he would look down with
adoring eyes on her whom he worshipped from afar. But
there had been a time, long ago, when he had known
her, out in a little village in Normandy, when they were
boy and girl together and had plighted their love one to
the other—but that was long ago. Her beauty had
attracted the attention of a wealthy patron, and now she
was the idol of Paris, and he—alas !

Night after night he had sat in the gallery looking
with hungry eyes upon her beauty, and when the play
was over had he not haunted the door to see her passing
out ? And then how he would hurry home and seize
his pen and write—so hard, so long—in the still and
silent watches of the night, write some strange, immortal
thing, and even as he wrote would sometimes fall asleep
and dream it was accepted—dream of the temple of
fame on the golden heights of Parnassus, dream of the
crown of laurel and the throne where he sat enthroned
in glory, with her, the queen of love and beauty, by his
side.

And he too, had written a play—a play for her to act.
It was rejected, and now what did the papers say ?

Eugene had gained the day. Eugene was famous :
Eugene was beloved. Eugene, Eugene, Eugene ! How
the name grated on his soul ! He heard it wherever he
went. The fame of his rival was the shadow that dark-
ened his life.

"They will come before the curtain," he muttered, with a picture of his rival's triumph in his eye. "They will come before the curtain, he and she, and stand together, hand-in-hand, and bow, he and mademoiselle. *Mon Dieu!*"

He buried his face in his hands and sat for a moment with the shadows deepening around him.

"It must not be," he muttered. "It must not be."

How to prevent it—that was the problem. How could he, a poor, unknown author, with barely enough to buy a ticket for the top gallery of the theatre—how could he prevent the performance of a play at one of the greatest operas in Paris?

He rose to light a lamp, and as he did so the flame flashed on the paper which lay on the table before him, and he read : "Fatal Accident ! Monsieur Droit of the Theatre Francais met with a fatal accident yesterday when crossing the bridge on the Seine. His foot slipped and he fell into the river. The body has not yet been recovered."

Monsieur Droit. Where had he seen that name? Ah yes, it was in the play bill. He was to have taken the part of the headsman in the play of Eugene Morell—Mary of Scots.

The author leaped to his feet with a sudden cry of delight. He knew the stage manager at the theatre; there was a vacancy in the company now, so he might face Eugene yet.

"Who says I cannot conceive a great idea ?" he cried in ecstasy. "Ah, it is sublime. What a drama it would make! But I will act this one myself. The ax—that I must arrange."

Seizing his hat he passed out of the room, down the stairs, and walked hurriedly in the direction of the theatre.

.   , ...

Eugene Morell pinned a rose to his coat and glanced approvingly at the mirror. He felt very happy that night, and the face reflected in the mirror was young and handsome and the eyes were beaming brightly with the unmistakable light of genius. The long days of his probation were over. He had found fame while yet in his youth, and was great in the flower of his days. His name was on all lips, his books delighted the eyes of millions. To-night he felt divine, and the ruby blood of the immortals pulsed in his veins. His masterpiece would to-night be played in the greatest theatre in Paris by the loveliest actress in France.

"The carriage is waiting, sir," said the maid, knocking at the door.

"Ah, yes, I'm coming," he answered gaily, and running down the stairs he leaped into the carriage and drove to the theatre like a king to his coronation.

.   .   .   .

The curtain rose. The eyes of a vast audience which filled every seat in the theatre were strained eagerly forward and fixed with anxious expectation on the stage.

Like some sweet fairy princess robed in garments of light and shedding a halo of beauty around her as she walked, she passed across the stage. Mary the Queen, Marie the beloved of the pauper. A vision of beauty forever it seemed to them, who say that she had never looked as beautiful as then, when on the strange and tragic night she played a part written for her alone by one whose inspiration was her love.

The first act was over and the curtain fell amid a hurricane of applause. The second and the third were repetitions of the first. With flushed cheeks the author sat in his box and beheld the triumph of his play, feeling how small a portion of the credit was due to him alone. He could not see the figure of his rival lurking in ghastly disguise behind the scenes, nor could he hear the whispered words which passed between the headsman and the Queen. .

"You or he!" muttered the headsman fiercely. "See, I have a revolver; warn him and he dies. And this is the ax for you! Choose, Marie. I swear it. You or he."

She shuddered and looking lovingly at the bouquet of flowers in her hand, the beautiful flowers Eugene had thrown at her feet.

"Ah! I love him," she cried passionately, as her eyes flashed fire at the gloomy figure before her. "Let it be me."

He trembled and bowed his head. "False," he muttered, "false."

The curtain rose. This was the last sad act. See, she was coming, the Queen, coming to the scaffold to die.

Why did she shudder as she walked up the steps of the scaffold—Sweet Marie. It was only a play after all. And yet how very realistic was that splendid tear in her eye as she turned and waved a last farewell to—strange she had waved it to one of the boxes. A mistake, pardonable in one who made so few.

A cold shiver ran through the frame of Eugene Morell as he leaned heavily on the side of his box, oppressed by a strange premonition of some hidden, inexplicable evil. What was it? See! The headsman! Ah, what eyes -— so cruel! How they glared! Now at him—now at her. Who was it?

How pale she was and how fair, as she mounted the steps of the scaffold—Sweet Marie—as she mounted the steps of the scaffold and waved a last farewell.

.   .   .   .

"Stop!" shrieked the author suddenly, as the ax swung through the air above her bended head.

It fell, and even as she smiled at him and waved a kiss—she died.

A cry of horror burst from the crowd, and then the curtain fell and he sat alone with his fame.

Toronto, June, 1896.

A Memory.

"IS it not beautiful?" she murmured, glancing through half-closed eyes around her.

The softened rays from colored lamps around were reflected in red and yellow flashes from the diamonds and the rubies on her neck. Her complexion was a beautiful pink delicately dusted with magnesia and her deep blue eyes shone brightly through a haze of belladonna. Her pose was adapted to the environment.

"Beautiful, indeed," he answered absently, with a far-away look in his eyes.

She was thinking of the place, the hour, the opportunity. He was not thinking of her. His eyes, averted, glanced dreamily downward at a flower in his hand—a little flower which he had plucked from a plant that nestled half-hidden among the roses by his side—a small forget-me-not.

"One feels so lonely at times in a great house like this," she murmured thoughtfully.

Vaguely he realized that a critical moment had come. Things had been drifting this way for several months, and with all the ingenuity of her artful sex she had led him to this point, and why should he not be led? She was an heiress and he was poor. She had beauty, talent, and wealth. She was the most admired, the most desired in her set, and many men had vainly sought the hand which she had plainly let him see was voluntarily his. And now she was sitting beside him.

Her glance was tender and her words were inviting. He had only to say a word and wealth and beauty and ease were his, and yet—

How sweet that little flower looked as it nestled in his hand, as sweet as that sweet hour long ago when suddenly there arose before him a face and he had heard a voice which stirred his inmost heart with sudden passion for possession, and dreams of sweet companionship, and a love surpassing life. Where were those dreams to-day? Whose was that love? Had someone else forgotten, and he—could he forget?

He shivered slightly and rose to fix the blind. Outside the world looked cold and cheerless. The night was dark, the frost was on the ground and a bitter wind was moaning among the trees. Inside was luxury, light and ease, soft cushions, comfort, jewels and gold, and all that gold could buy—and yet—

He was a lover of luxury and his heart was filled with a perennial longing for the beautiful things of life. How pleasant it would be to be at ease on these soft cushions, and live a life of idleness and ease freed from the necessity for daily toil—the bitter struggle for existence. Yes, for such luxury as this he might forego his liberty, endure the minor penalties of matrimony, the loss of friends and freedom, the domestic trials, the noisy children, the cares, the grief, the woman—and yet—He was counting up the chances. On one hand were beauty, wealth and ease. On the other hand—a memory.

Why did they play that valse? How the sweet music thrilled his heart with passionate remembrance and regret and visions of dead days and vanished faces :

> Can you forget the hour
>   When first we met,
> For woman—wealth—or power—
>   Can you forget ?   ·

She wondered at his hesitance. Would he let the golden opportunity go by ? Would he reject what others vainly sought ? When wealth and beauty lay at his feet, would he spurn them both aside ? What dream withheld him ? What vision held him back ?

> Can you forget the hour,
>   Sweet hour when first we met ?
> The fair, unfading flower,
>   The sun that will not set—
>   Till you forget ?

He rose unsteadily to his feet. The woman looked at him wonderingly. She could not see the face behind the flowers. She could not see the past. She could not hear the voice that echoed in the vaulted halls of memory :

> Forget me not, my lover,
>   For treason breeds regret :
> Life passeth in an hour,
>   But love—can love forget ?

A mist of tears obscured his sig.it. He could not see her beauty—he could not see her gold.

"I will say good-night," he said.

"Is it good-bye ? " she murmured.

" O, yes, good-bye," he answered. Through an aisle of flaming roses they passed from the conservatory out into the splendid halls, filled with luxurious things and noble pictures. She glanced significantly at them as they passed, and he who loved the beautiful—he shuddered to forego them. She opened the door. Outside the night was dark and cheerless. Inside was beauty and wealth and ease; but with a little flower in his hand he passed out into the night.

The Devil and Mrs. Grundy.

SATAN.— How'dy do, Mrs. Grundy?

MRS. GRUNDY.—I'm feeling very good, thankie, but the world is awful bad, Mr. Satan.

SATAN.—A chronic complaint, Mrs. Grundy, but I'm delighted to see you recognize me. There are some who doubt my existence.

MRS. GRUNDY.—Indeed, but I don't, Mr. Satan. I'm too good a Christian for that. But I didn't believe it was you at first, when I saw your cigarette, for I says to myself: The devil isn't wicked enough to smoke a cig-arette. The tempting of Eve was bad enough, but cig-arettes is worse. O, Mr. Satan, how shockin'!

SATAN.—Ha! Ha! Ha! Don't be too hard on me, Mrs. Grundy. I'm only a merry fellow looking round for a chance to make people happy.

MRS. GRUNDY.—You ought to be ashamed of your-self, Mr. Satan, to be a-doin' of things like that.

SATAN.—What—do you call it a sin to be happy?

MRS. GRUNDY.—My goodness, gracious, yes. This is no time to be happy—it's salvation we're a-seeking of here.

SATAN.—And are you finding it, Mrs. Grundy?

MRS. GRUNDY.—Yes, thank the Lord, I've found it, but this rest is awful wicked. And oh! it's a terrible time I'm havin' a-reformin' of this world. A-reformin' and reformin' and reformin' of the world. Such a wicked world as it is, Mr. Satan.

SATAN.—That's rather hard on its Maker.

MRS. GRUNDY.—Well, maybe the Lord did the best he could, but I can't understand what he was a-thinkin' of when he made such a wicked world. If it wasn't for me and the Christian Endeavours and the W.C.T.U., it wouldn't be fit to live in. But we're fixin' things up, Mr. Satan, we're a-cleanin' and scrubbing, and investigatin' and tryin' to make it respectable like and decent.

SATAN.—And how are Mr. Grundy and the children?

MRS. GRUNDY.—My gracious, goodness me, I ain't got no time to think about them. I'm too busy a-reformin' of the world. But bless me, now I come to think on it, I believe they is sick, Mr. Satan. I was down in the prison, to-day, makin' some soup for that poor dear murderer that killed his old mother with an ax, and he was a-takin' of it so nicely, and me consolin' with him and him repentin' and preparin' to die nice and Christianlike, when in comes a man to the prison and yells : " Your husband's a-dying, Mrs. Grundy, and your children is sick with the fever." Then I goes down on my knees and prays : " Look after them, Lord," says I. " Oh ! look after me husband and childer, Lord, while I'm lookin' after the world."

SATAN.—And did they get well, Mrs. Grundy?

MRS GRUNDY.—Indeed I don't know, Mr. Satan. I'm too busy a-reformin' to ask.

SATAN.—It's about this reforming matter I desired to see you, madam. I am, as you are doubtless aware, the proprietor of an establishment fitted up at the beginning of time to accommodate a limited number of sinners of a very superior kind. But since the apothesis of you,

Mrs. Grundy, the sinners are coming in too quick, and the quality is visibly deteriorating.

MRS. GRUNDY.—Indeed I'm sending you all I can, Mr. Satan, and gracious me, there's a lot of them, what with the people as smoke, and the people as drink, and them as goes to the theatres, and them as reads Sunday newspapers, and them as stays out late o' nights, and them as chews, and them horrible boys as smokes cigarettes, and them struttin' jades as goes to the matinees—O my gracious me, but there's an orful pile on 'em, Mr. Satan, and I'm bustlin' them off and hustlin' them all the time and sendin' 'em all to you just as quick as I can, Mr. Satan.

SATAN.—But madam, permit me to tell you that the accommodation is limited. We have all the heathen of all ages down there already, all the inhabitants of the great civilization previous to the Christian era, including the Athenians, the ancient Romans, including such eminent men as Plato, Socrates, Horace, and others with whom you are doubtless not acquainted.

MRS. GRUNDY.—Indeed, no.   I don't associate with sich haythens.

SATAN.—And in addition to these we have many illustrious moderns—heretics, madam, who were sent down for thinking, having been previously burned by the church—these and many more—in fact the great majority of the people on earth who live in other than Christian countries, and now to these you are sending down the great majority of Christians for the most trivial offences.

MRS. GRUNDY—But my goodness me, I can't allow

them to stay here, Mr. Satan, to associate with the likes of me—hussies as goes to matinees and sich like,

SATAN.—But the old-time sinners are objecting, Mrs. Grundy, to the class you are sending down now.   You can readily appreciate why a sinner of the high intellectual standing of Socrates or Galileo or Bruno who has earned his infernal pre-eminence by a long series of intellectual crimes, crowned by a glorious martyrdom on earth, should hesitate to associate with some poor little creature who is sent down for attending a ballet.   Consider these things, Mrs. Grundy.

MRS. GRUNDY.—Well I ain't a-sending you any murderers or thieves or such like now, Mr. Satan ; them poor dears nearly always repents and we makes them pies before they dies and sends 'em nice and comfortable to heaven.   It's jist the really wicked people as smokes cigarettes and drinks beer, and stays out late at nights, and rides in the Sunday cars, and dances, and laughs and sings, and plays cards, and them hussies as goes to matinees—O, them is the wicked ones, Mr. Satan.   We're sendin' 'em all down to you, and I hopes you scarify them well, Mr. Satan, pour biiin' water on 'em and skin 'em alive, Mr. Satan.   Don't I wish I was down to see 'em squirmin' !

SATAN.—Indeed, Mrs. Grundy, w e haven't the heart to punish them ; they look so sad by the time you get through with them that even the devils weep to behold them and we try to make them merry down below.

MRS. GRUNDY.—O my goodness me, what wickedness ! what wickedness—Lands above ! I never dreamed hell was so terrible as that to make men merry; why, I thought you only tortured them. How can you be so sinful Mr. Satan ? I ain't a-going to speak to you no more.

SATAN.—O Mrs. Grundy, Mrs. Grundy, you have made such a hell out of earth that people are looking to me for heaven.

King Billy and St. Pat.

SCENE.—*Hades*: A sort of half-way house between hell and heaven.

[Enter King Billy from the east and St. Pat. from the west.]

ST. PAT.—Hullo!

KING BILLY.—Whither away?

ST. PAT.—I'm bound for heaven.

KING BILLY.—So am I.

ST. PAT.—We seem to be going in different directions.

KING BILLY.—I know I'm right because I met you. If it's heaven you're after you'd better turn round.

ST. PAT.—Ah! ye can't coax a saint into hell.

KING BILLY.—Ah! St. Pat., St. Pat., it's ashamed I am of ye. Here's you been preaching heaven all your life and when you die you don't know where to find it.

ST. PAT.—Faith, I know where to find it all right but I'm not going to show you the way. It's yourself should be ashamed of yourself, King Billy, hanging around here for a chance to sneak in when I open the gate.

KING BILLY.—It's better to be hanging round here than hanging in there, and that's what you'll be doing if you ever get in, St. Pat

ST. PAT.—It's better than roasting down in hell.

KING BILLY.—Faith, it is you that was roasted on earth, St. Pat. I made it so hot for your kind on earth you'll find it cool in hell.

ST. PAT.—It's not the heat I'd mind, me boy, but how can I go to a Protestant church ?

[Flourish of fifes and drums in the distance. Enter Patrick O'Toole from the west and Dennis Hennessey from the east.]

HENNESSEY.—Hullo ! Is it you, O'Toole?

O'TOOLE.—Faith, this can't be heaven, for Hennessey's here.

HENNESSEY.—If there's a twig of blackthorn growing around I'd be after ye with a stick.

ST. PAT.—Peace, peace, my fine fellows. It is sinful to use angry words. I'm surprised at you quarrelling like this !

O'TOOLE.—Faith, but your reverence would not be surprised if ye knew why I kilt him below. It was for the holy St. Pat.

HENNESSEY.—And me for King Billy.

O'TOOLE.—And there's more at that game below.

ST. PAT. (to King Billy.)—I'm surprised that such a fine looking fellow should get his head broke through the likes of you.

KING BILLY.—O you needn't complain about that, for you never allowed him to use it.

ST. PAT.—He used it a little for thinking, or it might have been broken for you.

KING BILLY.—He'll get some light into it now which he didn't have before.

ST. PAT.—It was your tongue that caused all the mischief on earth.

KING BILLY.—I'll use it for singing in heaven.

ST. PAT.—Then you'll have the place all to yourself.

O'Toole.—Ouch! don't I wish I was back on the snug little earth again with me poipe and me poteen.

Sound of fifes and drums in the distance.

King Billy.—Listen to the angels playing.

St. Pat.—Faith I know where hell is now.

O'Toole.—There's a smell o' poteen comin up from below. That must be heaven down there.

Hennessey.—" I'm after that same."

Exit Hennessey followed hastily by O'Toole.

St. Pat.—Ah, but it's pitiful to see such fine looking fellows quarrelling about us below. Ah, now that I look at ye closely, Billy, ye seem fairly decent yourself.

King Billy.—It's worse company than yours I've been in, St. Pat. Ye improve very much on acquaintance.

St. Pat.—Well! Well! Now that it's all over, Billy, and we're both of us out of the game, do you think we did wise to be quarrelling below? What was it all about anyway?

King Billy.—Were we too busy fighting to think?

St. Pat.—And now we're too busy thinking to fight, but I fought for the right.

King Billy.—And so did I.

St. Pat.—Well, we'll both of us go to the right.

They turn to the right and enter heaven arm-in-arm.

Jonah and the Whale.*

JONAH.—Where am I at? The place seems dark and treacherous, and not a single ray of light can I discover to guide my footsteps from the depths mysterious. I know not where I am, nor whither I am going. What shall I do? My body bids me rest. My spirit craves for light, I shall protest.

WHALE.—What's this that I have swallowed, this being oratorical, vociferous, full of complaints, desires, hopes, ambitions, who though he sleeps in depths remote from light cries out for the stars, and clamors for the sunshine, and manifests a yearning for divinity out of proportion to his strength. It seems to be a different sort of creature to those which uncomplainingly lie in the stomachs of whosoever desireth to consume them and fatten on the strength they dare not use. And yet to look at 'twas a dainty morsel, and little different from the other worms."

JONAH.—Methinks the universe wherein I lie is speaking, or it hath found a voice that speaketh for it. Oh, thou mysterious and tremendous being within whose depths cadaverous I am lying, inform me, I beseech you where I am and why and wherefore, and whither I am going?

WHALE.—Be quiet, or I'll digest you.

JONAH.—That is no way to argue. Give me reasons.

*The above dialogue has no reference to the scripture story of Jonah, but is purely symbolical.

WHALE.—What infidel, could you ask for reasons. O what impious morsel have I swallowed—a worm that asks for reasons lies uneasy in the stomach that seeks to fatten on the brains of men. O wicked worm adapt yourself to fate. Whatever is, must be, then why complain?

JONAH.—And if you looked to fate to feed you, whale, methinks you would not live to feed on man.

WHALE.—I am a great big whale, and you are only a little man. I help myself, but you depend on fate, but if you are an obedient little man I will be a generous whale and tell you pretty stories about the great sea, and the stars and gods—the things you seek but cannot find.

JONAH.—And will it be true, O whale?

WHALE.—On the word of a whale what I tell you is true—The world is a great big ball, consisting of the sea and the sky. In the sky is Providence and eternal joy, while the sea is inhabited by me, its representative, and a number of little men who are wicked and cannot swim. I swallow these men to save them from drowning, and the only way they can reach salvation is by passing through me, after which they enter heaven. Therefore be quiet, Jonah. On the word of a whale I swallowed you because I loved you and through me lies salvation.

JONAH.—O whale, methinks that your philosophy coincides extremely well with your desires. Your wisdom is begotten of your necessities, and your advice agreeth with your appetite.

WHALE.—Whatever is, must be. On the word of a

whale, it is the will of Providence that you lie where you lie.

JONAH.—And if it be the will of Providence that you lie when you lie, then Providence has given you a tongue that has betrayed you.   But even if your tongue had served you better, your appetite has revealed to me your grossness, and whoso entereth you, seeking salvation, findeth but darkness and destruction.

WHALE.—What is this that I have swallowed.   Methinks within his brain there lurks a poison that will destroy me.   Yea, with his talk he seems to feed upon me, gnawing his way to the light.   The brains of men, like fangs of serpents, must be destroyed by those who would feed upon them, else will they sting and slay. Begone, rash mortal.   I reject you—

Vomits him.

JONAH.—Ah, see the sun—how glorious.   The sea is deep, but swimming by myself, methinks I'll reach eternal shores while yon gross monster sinketh to the depths.

The Haunted Trolley.

"IT was here he fell," said the conductor. "Right under the wheels of the car ,and they went over him. I can hear his bones crunching, still sir, —eh ! did some one speak ?"

The car stopped abruptly as he hastily turned the brake.

"I heard a voice," said the conductor ; "did some one call ?"

There was silence on the car. The three passengers inside and the man on the platform looked at the questioner curiously and shook their heads. It was an all night car and the hour was nearly twelve. The conductor had been on duty all night. "Some one got on," said the conductor. "Ah, you got in, did you ? I thought I heard you call."

The number of passengers in the car was still the same. The bell rang twice and the conductor resumed his place on the platform. The passengers looked wonderingly around the car, but no remarks were passed. The car swept swiftly on its course till a couple of blocks farther, then it stopped and the outside passenger got off. The conductor re-entered the car.

"Fares, please."

The passengers paid their fares, and the conductor passed up the aisle to a vacant seat : and held out his box as to an invisible passenger—

"Fare, please."

There was a faint clink in the box. The passengers shivered and looked at the door. The conductor was looking steadily before him with a dazed look in his eyes.

"Transfer, did you say," he muttered. "We don't transfer to heaven."

There was silence again in the car. Silence. What was that? A whisper—what was it, the spectral sound that came from the vacant seat?

"I say we don't do it," repeated the conductor angrily, as though arguing with some invisible passenger. "It can't be done, I say."

There was silence again for a moment, then again that spectral sound, and a look of relief passed over the face of the conductor.

"To the cemetery," he muttered vaguely. "O, yes, I'll take you as far as the cemetery."

He turned and passed to the door. The passengers rose hastily to follow him, when suddenly he turned fiercely upon them. His face was ghastly pale and his eyes looked wildly before him filled with a great horror.

"Don't leave me," he muttered weakly. "Don't leave me alone with him.

They shivered.

"I told him a lie," he whispered hoarsely. "This car is not going to heaven. It is bound straight for hell."

They looked at him wonderingly.

"Do you know the reason why?" he asked. "Because I'm on it; that's why. It was me that killed him, you know. He loved her, and I ran over him instead of stopping the car."

The bell rang suddenly.

" He wants to get out !" shrieked the conductor. " This is the cemetery. Ha ! Ha ! Ha !"

The lights of the car went out suddenly. The passengers shrunk trembling against the sides. Out of the darkness a white hand shone with uplifted finger beckoning to the conductor. There was a sound as though some one was strugg'ing. Then the lights flashed up again and fell on the face of a corpse bent forward with wildly protruding eyes, and hand upon the brake.

Politics as a Fine Art.

The ditches are full of men who have written essays on "How to Succeed," but the lips of the gods are sealed.

Hence it follows that an essay on this subject, to be wise, must always be short, for he who knows how to succeed will never give it away, and he who gives it away will never succeed.

April 1, 1898.

Impressions of a Poet.

THERE is a subtle element in the works of this poet not found in the works of his predecessors. His genius seems of a finer and less material type than theirs. His verse throbs with a strange and mysti- cal music which sweeps in maddened ecstacy along the lines, and glows with a terrible intensity into a weird white passion, which dazzles all sense and strikes a new chord in the mind. Light, heat, energy, beauty, are all present in his verse, but to these there seems super- added a new and more subtle element which blends with and beautifies the rest, and into which they seem at times to pass. The poet seems at times to be swayed and tortured by some mighty inspira- tion which he can indicate but not express. Innumer- able harmonies mingle in his verses and blend into musical colours, which dazzle as well as entrance ; and beneath the restless surface of the enchanted sea there seems to rage and tremble a mighty undercurrent. The musical waves keep time to a vast undertone, and swell like echoes of wild spirit voices singing an anthem in the soul's deep sea. From the vaults and the valleys of the spirit-haunted mind there flows sad strains of music weirdly beautiful. The reader is moved by a sense of haunting melodies, of light and shadow, strangely ming- ling, of invisible presences haunting the valleys of space, of brooding spirits hovering in the vaults of the mid- night, of purple rivers flowing through the veins of the air, of strange hurryings to and fro of invisible feet, of babblings of angel voices in a strange and mystical universe which the wand of the poet has made near.

And yet it was in the mind that these things had their being. Nature never changed her form at the bidding of the poet. He clothed her in a new and radiant garment. The marvellous images which he has crystallized in verse were not reflections of the world without, but were revelations of the world within. It was in the mind's deep universe that the maddened music had its home, and there, too, were the tremulous shadows of thought, the shifting lights of love, the burning passions of the self-torturing soul, the sublime cognition of an eternal truth, the varying visions of a spirit world, the changing chimes of innumerable bells hung in the belfry of the intellect, the trumpet call of a beleaguered truth, the war between the powers of night and light, the vast darkness that at time prevailed and clothed the ideas in crape before sending them forth to the world, and behind the darkness, like the sun behind the night, a radiant and beautiful soul which wore its sorrow like a veil, and ever and again ordained deep silence in the mind, recalled the militant ideas, absorbed all modes and music, and in the ecstasy of deep introspection realized itself as the eternal Ego.

Extraordinary Episode.

THERE is a mysterious restaurant in the city where steaks are fried all night, and where, while the ordinary people of the city are sleeping the sleep of the guilty, the elect of the gods foregather together to discuss the eternal verities in language both extraordinary and divine.

I had heard of this restaurant mysterious from one who had never been there. The fame of its steaks was whispered abroad, and its dinners were greatly renowned. Its port had no rival in Eblis, and its sherry was never surpassed, and it was darkly said that those whose money bags were large could coax from its cellar subterranean some of the divinest Pommery that ever drove care from the heart of a cynic, or kindled splendid lightning in the soul.

What wonder then that returning home one night from a function abnormally late, curiosity united with hunger led me to the door where a bright light brightly burning told me that steaks were frying and waiters, forever sleepless, were ready to serve me within the doors of the restaurant mysterious.

. . . .

I took a seat at a table in a compartment by myself and a spectral-looking waiter glided softly to my side and placed the menu before me, but I laid it to one side and told him to bring me steak. He glided softly away, and I sat with the menu beside me awaiting his return. The room was small, but exquisitely furnished and

panelled in mahogany and oak, with mirrors set in the
wall.   The light of the coloured gasalier, and softened
and subdued, and the atmosphere abnormally warm, was
delicately perfumed with an odour of violet and musk,
which stole into the senses, filling the heart and spirit
with a delicate perfumed joy.   It may have been the
lateness of the hour, or possibly the glamour of the
surroundings and abnormal warmth of the room, coming
in sharp reaction after the frosty air outside, which
disposed my senses to slumber, and caused me to close
my eyes.   When I opened them again, in a moment, I
was somewhat startled to find a stranger seated before
me, his face faintly outlined in the shadows at the dark
side of the table, and his bright eyes fixed intently on
my face, with the strangest look in the world.   The
waiter glided into the room again, and passed away like
a shadow, leaving a steak on the table before me.   I
lifted my knife to cut it.

" Don't ! "

Like a beautiful note of music the word fell on my
ear from the lips of the stranger before me.   I lifted my
eyes and looked at him wonderingly, and then, for the
first time, I observed that he was beautiful—as beautiful as the dawn.   His face was that of a youth barely
out of his teens ; flawless as that of Antinous, with
eyebrows arched, and tremulous, sensitive lips, and eyes
that flashed like stars.

" Is it poisoned ? " I asked wonderingly, looking from
him to the steak.

" Yes, poison," he answered musically.   " It is steak."
"Why poison ?" I insisted.

" Earth, would you feed the earth ?" he cried impatiently. " Whatever food you add to your body adds to the burden of clay on your soul and makes you less divine."

The remark, if extraordinary, impressed me as being sublime and quite in harmony with an environment where the hum-drum remarks of everyday life may never profane the ear. I looked at the menu again.

" If you will pardon the divinity of the remark," I answered gaily. " But where on the menu of mortality can you find the elixir celestial to kindle spiritual fires ?"

His bright eyes flashed divinely, and he leant forward in his chair till his soft breath fanned my face and his purple lips said softly: " I can give you what you will if you will give a soul to me. I am Satan."

I looked at him for a moment more in wonderment than fear, then sudden'y burst out laughing, it seemed so infernally funny to be sitting there with Satan, a gentleman whose fame is as wide as the wor'd —whose achievements are written in history both secular and divine, and whose career was so very romantic that many have doubted its reality. I had never dreamed he was so beautiful, but seeing him before me here to-night with his wonderful eyes flashing fire, and his purple lips aflame with eloquence, I could readily appreciate the charm of a personality which tempted Eve in Eden and tempted me to-night.

" Will you sell me your soul ?" he whispered.

" Ah, my beautiful tempter," I answered, laughing gaily, " if it were any soul but my own—but really."

" It is yours I want," he said. " The others are too ordinary."

"Whom the gods wish to destroy they first delight, saith the proverb, and whom Satan desires to possess he flatters. The remark put me on my guard.

"Will you sell me your soul?" he cried.

"Have you been to the Klondike?" I asked.

"No, the climate is too chilly," he said, with a merry laugh; "but I have resources of my own, and if you consider for a moment you will see that the soul is useless to you in a practical world like this, where beauty, and sweetness, and light, and love are held to be lower than gold. I can appreciate it—give it to me."

There was truth in what he said, and I remembered that the divinest things I had written had been the least appreciated.

"But if the world is sordid," I answered, "all the more need for my beautiful soul to console me for its folly. I will not sell my soul."

"Ah, thank you," he answered gaily, arising to his feet. "I thank you for refusing, for the only things worth having are the ones we cannot buy. You will no sell, but you can give. I am not that mythical Satan who exists only in priestly dreams, invented by the fathers of error to frighten people to their knees. Listen! I am Lucifer."

His voice was softest music, and his bright eyes flashed divinely. His glances shot sweet lightnings through my veins, filling me with a sense of sublime illumination, and thrilling my soul with exquisite melodies. His eyes shone like sweet stars, and brightly outlined in the shadows about him I seemed to see a golden aureole round his brow.

" I am Lucifer—angel of light—once the first of the angels of heaven—now banished.   I was beautiful, and they envied me.   I was proud, and they hated me.   In twilight of evenings celestial I walked on the outermost battlements and looked down and pitied mankind, and then I was banished from heaven, but I shall return. again.   Will you come?"

His breath clung close to mine, and thrilling me with divinity, and seeming to suck my soul from my body into his.

" The bell is ringing for celestial suppers.   Let us go forth and greet the gods together."

    .   .   .   .

" Your steak is getting cold, sir."

I looked up in wonder.   The waiter was standing before me.

" Where is Lucifer?" I said.   " Did you hear the beautiful angel?"

" I think you have been sleeping, sir," he said.   " Perhaps you were talking to yourself."

I laughed.

City Celestial.

ONE night when the world was a-sleeping,
  And I lay all alone in my bed,
My spirit was filled with a yearning
  To seek for the souls of the dead.

And all of a sudden the darkness
  Was thrilled by a murmur of wings,
By mystical vo:ces and visions,
  And a strain like the tugging of strings :
And my spirit crept out of my body,
  And left it alone on the bed,
And I swept from the shadows terrestrial.
  On the paths that are trod by the dead,
To the gates of a city celestial,
  A city sublime and divine.

O, hark to the cymbals celestial,
  How they tingle and quiver and ring !
How they shiver, and tingle, and quiver,
  And tingle, and shiver, and ring !

Sweet music, sweet incense, sweet laughter,
  Sweet flowers, sweet rapture, sweet light,
Sweet living, sweet loving, sweet singing.
  Sweet love, sweet joy, sweet light.

Sweet spirit celestially singing, sweet cymbals
  celestially ringing,

Sweet seraphs celestially flinging, from censors
  celestially swinging
  The sweet celestial light.
Sweet swinging, sweet swinging, sweet swinging
  Sweet singing, sweet singing, sweet singing,
Sweet anthems celestially ringing
  Through halls celestially bright

Then I trembled and shivered and quivered
  With wild divine delight,
With rapture of loving and living,
  Sweet joy, sweet peace, sweet light,
And I stretched out my arms to the city,
  And I cried, " Let me in – let me in.
  An heir to the kingdom immortal
Hath come to the heavenly portal.
  Let me in—let me in—let me in."

O, hark to the cymbals celestial,
  How they tingle and quiver and ring,
How they shiver and tingle and quiver,
And tingle and shiver and ring.

Sweet music, sweet incense, sweet laughter,
  Sweet flowers, sweet rapture, sweet light
Sweet living, sweet loving, sweet singing,
  Sweet love, sweet joy, sweet light.

Sweet spirit celestially singing, sweet cymbals
  celestially ringing.
Sweet seraphs celestially flinging, from censors
  celestially singing,

The sweet celestial light.
Sweet swinging, sweet swinging, sweet swinging,
Sweet singing, sweet singing, sweet singing,
Sweet anthems celestially ringing
Through halls celestially bright.

Still I stretched out my arms to the city
    And I cried—let me in, let me in—
"I am tired of hoping and dreaming
    Of seeking, and serving and scheming
In the shadowy realm terrestrial,
I am heir to the kingdom celestial
    Let me in, let me in, let me in.

"O, who is this mortal immortal
    Who out of the darkness hath fled
To kneel at the heavenly portal?
    Is he dead—is he dead—is he dead?
On the wings of a vision celestial
    He hath crept through the fingers of fate.
In the halls of the kingdom terrestial
    Let him wait—let him wait, let him wait,
Till the voice of the angels celestial
    Hath summoned him back to the gate."

   ·   ·   ·   ·   ·   ·

And now I am sitting in darkness,
    I sit in the shadows and wait,
A spirit, a beautiful spirit,
    I sit in the prison of fate
Till the angels come down in the darkness
    And summon me back to the gate.

   ·   ·   ·   ·   ·

O city, sweet city celestial,
  Sweet city, sublime and divine,
Where the lips of the loved to the lover
  Cling close as the blood to the vine.
Some day I shall pass from the shadows
  Where I tremble and shiver and wait.
From the depths of the darkness terrestial
  I shall pass to the city celestial,
And God will throw open the gate.
  And forever and ever and ever
I shall reign in its halls like a king,
  And forever and ever and ever
I shall join with the angels who sing—
And the cymbals that tingle and quiver,
  And tingle and quiver and ring !
And shiver, and tingle, and quiver,
  And tingle, and shiver, and ring !

Sweet music, sweet incense, sweet laughter,
  Sweet flowers, sweet rapture, sweet light.
Sweet living, sweet loving, sweet singing,
  Sweet love, sweet joy, sweet light.

Sweet spirit celestially singing, sweet cymbals
  celestially swinging,
Sweet seraphs celestially flinging, from censors
  celestially singing,
  The sweet celestial light.
Sweet swinging, sweet swinging, sweet swinging,
  Sweet singing, sweet singing, sweet singing,
Sweet anthems celestially ringing
  Through halls celestially bright.

Something.

HE threw the book aside, for his spirit was tired of shadows and filled with a wonderful longing for something which books could not give—something—something—something—a beautiful, passionate Something—not found in the pages of books.

He picked up his pen and looked at it curiously. This was the weapon with which he must conquer the world and woo the affections of men. This was the tool of his craft, with which he would record the delicate contrivances of thought and weave into a crown those mental jewels ; those intellectual delicacies ; those precious pearls thrown from the soul's deep sea ; those flaming thoughts forged in the spirit's fire ; those subtle strains of music sweet and splendid which trembled in golden chords on the melodious soul—the little pen would tell them all to men, and from its quivering point the hot electric stream of pain and passion, love and joy and sorrow, in lava streams of many-hued emotion, would pass forth to the world and win him something—something—something—a passionate, beautiful Something not found in the pages of books.

He walked to the window and looked out. There was the world, his kingdom or his grave—the beautiful, hideous world, the temple of delight and home of misery, the battle-field and resting-place of all—out there the fight was going on, the everlasting fight of strength and weakness, truth and falsehood, light and darkness. The faint east wind that fanned his face brought to his ears the sound of many voices—the voices of men and women and little children—happy voices, woeful voices, cruel voices, gentle voices, groans and laughter, joy and sorrow, strangely blended out there in the battle-field of life. Why was he lingering in his study when the fight was on? He must go out and struggle with them, for there perhaps among the toiling millions—perhaps in a cottage, perhaps in a palace, out on the stormy sea maybe, or in some quiet valley, in the heat of the battle or in the peace beyond the storm—he might find that something—something—something—the passionate, beautiful Something he could not find in books.

The perfume of the flowers of the world came sweetly on the breeze towards him, filling his heart with the passion and fever of living; the wish, the desire and the craving to venture out and pluck each little flower in the roseate garden of the world—to pluck and kiss each perfect little flower, to deck himself with all the flowers of joy. The shadows of the study were behind him, the joys of life before. His many-colored soul was all aflame with passionate desire for life and joy; and far beyond the dreaming and the toiling, sweet-thrilling on the surface of the breeze, he hears the voice and sees the eyes of something—something—something—a passionate, beautiful Something not found in the pages of books.